Dubicki's

Gabriella Scott

Cover Design by Regina Wamba:
www.MaeIDesign.com

Editing by Patrick and April Durham:
www.editingandebooks.com

ISBN-13: 978-1-7320375-7-1

ISBN-10: 1-7320375-7-4

DUBICKI'S

1

Jason Rourke loved mornings. Each day when he woke and caught a glimpse of the sunlight streaming through the crack in his window shades, he knew it was a new day filled with new opportunities. He was not discouraged that today it was a short glimpse of the sun on what was a cloudy autumn day. As one of the top real estate developers in Minneapolis, he had to stay on top of things. The best deals started in the mornings.

He looked out his 30th floor condominium at the beautiful skyline of Minneapolis, Minnesota. His family had moved here from Chicago when he was a kid, and they still talked about Chicago like it was home. For him, Minneapolis was his pride and joy. His dad still loved to tease him on Sundays when the whole family was cheering for the Chicago Bears and Jason was always wearing his Vikings jersey. Jason had always argued that he'd grown up here and bled purple, the primary color of the Vikings. They had come to love their sports rivalry over the years.

Jason had gone to college locally and started as a real estate agent right after graduating. At the time, real estate was booming. All you had to do was breathe, pass your real estate exam, and stand in a real estate office. The clients would come to you faster than you could take them. Life was good.

In 2008, the American economy started a fiscal down turn, and the mortgage crisis caused a shift in the real estate business. A shift that caused a decrease to the sizeable income Jason had been accustomed to making. Jason was still motivated to succeed and shifted his focus within the market. Along with selling real estate, he started investing in it. This evolved into establishing his own real estate company, Rourke Real Estate. Now he was one of the leading real estate development firms in the city.

Jason was on the verge of making one of the sweetest deals of his career. There was a block of residences and businesses in northeast Minneapolis that were on prime land to build a high rise right near the Mississippi River. He just had to convince the last two property owners to sell. It had been easy to convince the other residences on the block to sell. Many of them had wanted to move but were not able to get the value that they wanted from selling in this economy. Rourke Real Estate helped them with that and paid them a premium they would not have otherwise had for their properties. The local businesses on the block had been another story.

Now he was faced with a bar and a butcher shop, both having been in the neighborhood for at least fifty years. He almost had an agreement with the butcher shop because of the size of the payment they were being offered. They hadn't liked it at first, but now they were hearing numbers that made them consider the offer seriously. The last place he truly had to contend with was Dubicki's, a bar that had been built by and maintained by the Dubicki family for three generations. Closing this deal wouldn't be easy, but Jason hadn't earned his stellar reputation the easy way. He prided himself in hearing the word "no" as a challenge and would find a way to get this done.

He walked over to his Keurig coffee machine and

chose his favorite Italian roast. He picked up his remote control to the stereo system that was wired throughout his entire home and chose one of his favorite opera composers, Puccini. He liked rock and roll like most other men, but, in the mornings, there was nothing like the heavenly sounds of opera to start the day.

After the hour he always took for his morning routine, he emerged from his sizeable walk-in closet in a suit and tie, looking like the well-dressed real estate mogul that he was. It was going to be a good day.

2

Kelsey hated mornings. Her late night job conflicted with having the routine of a normal workday and always made getting out of bed the next day difficult. The consolation was the timer on the coffee maker and the sweet aroma coming from the kitchen telling her that a rescue was on its way.

Six months ago, Kelsey had to drop out of the Minneapolis Institute's College of Art and Design to help her brother Adam with the family business. Her father had died of a heart attack the year before and left his bar in northeast Minneapolis to his children. Her mother had died when she was a child, so, when her dad died, it was just her and her two brothers. Her youngest brother, Jesse, had dreams of being a mixed martial arts fighter and, at 22, was not ready to give up his dreams. They were a tightknit group of siblings, and, on Jesse's dreams, they all agreed. Kelsey decided that, as the middle child, she should step up to the plate and put her dream of being an illustrator for children's books on hold for now.

As the months of working late nights at the bar passed, it wore on Kelsey more each day. Her father instilled a strong work ethic in all of his children, though. She took most of the closing shifts to help Adam because he had a family. They'd agreed that there should be one of them present at the bar at all times. This meant she had to balance the cash register and stock the bar. Add to that the drunk guys who had a hard time leaving and usually hit on her in their drunken slurs by offering to buy her shots. As if that would ever happen. Sometimes she didn't get out of there until 5 a.m., and she'd have to start all over again early the next afternoon.

The only thing that kept her going was supporting Jesse's dreams of being a professional MMA fighter. Since she'd had to put her own dreams on hold, she wanted to support her baby brother. Kelsey and Jesse had always been the closest of the three because they had been born within two years of each other. Her relationship with Jesse and her best friend Mimi were the two things that she had that she truly valued besides helping the family business. She could afford her own dreams later. For now, she had to step up to the plate and support her family.

She shuffled her legs to the coffee maker like a zombie. This was going to be another long day.

3

Jason was not discouraged by the dreary November weather. It had been a warm autumn, and in Minnesota that was a blessing. There could very easily be snow on the ground, so he was happy with a little bit of rain and warmer temperatures for that time of year. He cruised down Central Avenue and across the Third Street Bridge in his black Cadillac Escalade. As the sounds of Jimi Hendrix flowed through the car, he thought about how he was going to pitch to the last business on the block that wouldn't budge at his previous offers. Listening to good music always inspired Jason. He could talk his way around any issue that caused a sentimental owner not to want to sell. With money plus his negotiation skills, he felt unstoppable.

Dubicki's was a well-established bar and restaurant in northeast Minneapolis. The original population of that part of the city had been primarily Polish and Ukrainian, but the housing boom ten years ago had driven people into the city, bringing more diversity. Bars and restaurants grandfathered in around current zoning laws sat side-by-side with houses on residential streets. Thus, establishments like Dubicki's were popular with long-standing members of the community, as well as with neighborhood bar crawls, bachelorette parties, and other special events. It drew in lots of people from all around the Twin Cities of Minneapolis and St. Paul. A year ago, Frank Dubicki had died leaving the bar to his children. Now the oldest son owned it. Adam Dubicki ran the business and would not sell out of the principle of sentiment for his family and all that they'd built.

Jason stepped into the door of the old brick building and brushed the rain off of his shoulders. It was late morning, 10 a.m., and there was enough time before lunch for him to speak with Adam Dubicki. He observed the establishment around him. Other than a few people bellied up to the bar that he assumed to have been regulars, the place was pretty quiet. Adam came out from the back, his jaw set in a defensive manner. He greeted Jason with wariness and suspicion in his eyes.

"Hello, Mr. Dubicki," Jason said with a smile, extending his hand.

Adam didn't accept it.

"Listen, Mr. Rourke, we've been over this several times. Nothing has changed. I told you. We're not selling. End of story."

"I understand that you have a family history here, and you want to uphold your family tradition. I respect that. I am willing to generously compensate you for selling so that you can rebuild an even better establishment. Ultimately, you will be able to grow the Dubicki's legacy for future generations."

"There's no amount of money that could get us to leave this building. My grandfather's father helped *build* this building. That's part of the reason my grandfather chose to start a business here." At age 29, Adam Dubicki had a pretty good head for business, and his loyalty to his family ran deep. Adam was also convinced that even if they were to sell that he'd probably be haunted by three generations of Dubicki men.

"Think of all the future generations you could provide a legacy for with the one million dollars you are being offered," Jason told him. "We could even make retaining the original bricks part of the agreement so you would have those bricks to be rebuild with," said Jason.

Adam really didn't like this arrogant prick. He wasn't going to sell that easy, but he owed it to his wife and siblings to call a family meeting to tell them what they were being offered. Adam may have been the owner-in-name, but they were a family. As a family, they would all agree to sell, or they would all agree to fight. There was no in-between.

4

"No way!" Kelsey exclaimed.

Kelsey and her best friend Mimi had decided to get in some early Christmas shopping. They had detoured to the lingerie department, and Mimi's dramatic flair had her suggesting items that were a little too risqué for Kelsey.

"Kelsey, you've got to live a little if we are ever going to get you out there again," Mimi told her. "I know your breakup with Zeke broke your heart, but that was a year ago. They aren't all losers like him."

Hearing Mimi say his name made Kelsey emotional. Two years ago, Zeke had bumped into her in the parking lot one day after class. They were in their first year of school at MCAD. All of her papers went flying, and he'd helped her get back to her car. There was an instant chemistry between them. He had asked her to coffee, and one thing had led to another.

They'd had a passionate relationship for six months. Every time Kelsey was near Zeke her breathing got shallow as she felt the excitement of being near him. One day, she decided to surprise him at his apartment and heard moans behind the door. She'd just assumed it was his player of a roommate, Ted. As she opened the door, she was horrified. There was Zeke in the throes of passion with a person she thought was one of her better friends, Brittany. Kelsey had frozen for a moment, watching them, before she turned and ran out the door. Zeke had tried to chase her and explain, but she'd never looked back. Her dreams of a future and a family were shattered that day.

"Hello? Where are you, Kelsey? You have that look in your eyes that says that you might be torturing yourself over Zeke again," said Mimi apprehensively.

"I don't know, Mimi. I just don't think I'm ready to get out there again. I work odd hours and now don't even go to school anymore. Why would any guy want to date me, anyway? Maybe I'll just get a couple of cats and become a crazy cat lady. Then I'll learn to knit, and we can call it a day. No man will ever want to touch me."

"Oh, come on! Let me get out my violin and play you a sad song. You're only 24, and your life is far from over. Now, let's find a compromise in the lingerie department. You're not getting out of here without a sexy bra and panties. My treat. They'll make you *feel* sexy. That, my friend, makes everything better."

Kelsey sighed and gave in. Once Mimi had an idea in her head, she usually got her way. That girl had a fierce stubborn streak! Mimi also had the kind of beauty that women envy. She had long, dark hair that curled just perfectly when she wanted. She possessed an alluring, exotic look that made discerning her ethnicity a mystery. Her gorgeous café-colored complexion, paired with all the right curves, made her so beautiful she was almost intimidating. Mimi just didn't seem to understand that not everyone turned a man's head the way that she did.

Kelsey felt like the girl next door. Especially next to Mimi. Kelsey was about 5' 5" and had always been a bit of a tomboy. Growing up, she had played sports to keep up with her brothers. Her athletic build suited her thicker frame. She wasn't stick-skinny and was okay with that. Her large bust was a little more than she wanted, but she did her best to hide that with big sweaters and turtlenecks in the winter. In true tomboy style, she usually kept her reddish brown hair up in a ponytail so she didn't have to fool with it, and she wasn't really big on makeup. Just a little bit of lip gloss and she was all set for the day. She also never understood the fuss Mimi made about fashion. Still, Kelsey figured she would just go along with Mimi's scheme to bring out Kelsey's sexy side, even if she nearly laughed at the thought of having one. She'd decide what to do with the fancy underwear when she got home. That way they could get on with their Christmas shopping and keep on task.

Kelsey loved that Christmas decorations were up everywhere. She loved the feeling that the holidays were in the air. Last year, she had started her own tradition of buying a special ornament for her Christmas tree. She had gotten the cutest little lamb sleeping on a cloud and wondered what might possibly top it this year.

Mimi squealed in delight as they passed a jewelry store, and Kelsey laughed. Mimi never was able to resist anything that sparkled.

"I'm just going to go to that Christmas store a few stores over while you check out the jewelry, okay?" Kelsey said.

Mimi barely heard her but acknowledged Kelsey's choice with an "Okay."

As Kelsey entered the store, she was overcome by the magic that was Christmas. Bing Crosby sang "White Christmas" as she savored walking slowly through the displays. When she was younger and both her parents were still alive, Christmas was a magical time in their home. Unfortunately, her mother died of breast cancer when Kelsey was eight. After her mother passed away, decorations around the Dubicki house had become scarce. Her parents had a love that people only read about, and her dad had never been the same after her mother died. Kelsey had hoped her dad would stay around for longer than he did. Her only consolation was hoping that her parents were together in Heaven, somewhere.

Since she'd moved out, Kelsey had started putting up her own tree every year to make up for the time lost doing so as a child. She had a little apartment that was the top level of a duplex in the Audobon Park neighborhood of northeast Minneapolis. It wasn't far from work or where she grew up, and it was on the side of town that people from the suburbs had moved into a few years ago during the housing boom. The neighborhood had the perfect blend of old and new, and she loved it. It was perfect for her. One of Adam's friends had bought the house just over a year ago and wanted to rent the upstairs to someone he knew he could trust. At the time, Kelsey had just broken things off with Zeke. She wanted to get as far away from her place uptown near Zeke's as possible, and it had felt good to move home to the side of the city that she belonged.

Her apartment had just one bedroom, lots of sunlight, and enough space for a cute little kitchen table. She'd put cute café style curtains on the kitchen windows, and she loved sitting at that table drinking coffee before she got ready for work each day. She also had a small desk in the living room for when she wanted to write. She found the process of journaling cathartic since her break-up with Zeke. Mimi was right, though. Kelsey needed to move on. Making an effort to do just that, she started to imagine all the ways she'd make her home feel even cozier when she got out her Christmas décor next week on the day after Thanksgiving. The holidays always brought her joy and renewed her hope for the future.

Kelsey spotted the perfect ornament for this year: a beautiful angel with a trumpet. She loved the detail of the angel's face. It was sculpted so closely she felt as if she were almost seeing through the eyes of God. It reminded her of an angel proclaiming the birth of Christ. She knew she had to have it. As she was checking out her purchase, her cell phone rang.

"Hello?"

"Kelsey, it's Adam. We need to have a family meeting tonight. I got Mike to cover your shift at the bar. Jesse's coming and so is Stephanie."

Kelsey wondered what was wrong. It had to be pretty major for her younger brother Jesse to cancel MMA practice at the gym. Stephanie was Adam's wife and was usually at home taking care of their six-month-old, Jack.

"Adam, what's going on? You've never called a family meeting like this. Is everything okay?"

"Everything is fine, Kels. Don't worry. I've just been approached by a real estate developer about the land that our bar is on. I have no intention of selling but thought we should meet as a family to decide if we want to consider what the guy is offering."

Kelsey got so mad she nearly raised her voice until she remembered she was in a public place. Her father had called her feisty more than once due to her inability to control her temper or opinions when they were challenged.

"You aren't seriously considering this, are you, Adam? Dad would roll over in his grave, not to mention Dziadek."

Dziadek was the Polish term for Grandfather. Her dad's father hadn't spoken a lot of English, so they'd learned to talk to him in the language of the old country. Kelsey was the most fluent of the three grandchildren, but both her brothers called her grandfather Dziadek, as her dad would have it no other way. Dziadek died when she was fifteen, but she would never forget his rosy cheeks and the way he would always dance with her when she was a little girl. He'd twirl her around and make her laugh. He could talk to anybody. She'd loved her Dziadek. That bar was his pride and joy; built by his father before him after her great-grandparents had moved here from Poland. Starting his own business was her grandfather's American Dream.

"Kelsey, settle down. Of course I'm not seriously considering it, but I have to tell you guys what's been going on so you know. And I have to give it a vote because this company is offering a substantial amount. I'll tell you more tonight. Have a little faith, okay?"

Kelsey acquiesced and told Adam she'd be there. She knew if she ever ran into the man that wanted to take Dubicki's, however, she'd give him a piece of her mind.

5

Jason entered the mall to meet a potential investor for coffee. He hated going into shopping malls but would do anything for business. As he sat down with his cup of steaming coffee, his eyes were drawn to two young women walking past him.

One was gorgeous. The kind of girl you might see on a magazine cover. She had an exotic look to her. The kind of girl he thought he could have fun with, but not much more. He'd been there, done that. The other girl with her had an absolute fire in her eyes. He was intrigued by whatever it was that fueled her anger. He was glad she couldn't kill with that look, but he really wanted to know what had put the bee in her bonnet.

She had the kind of modest beauty that said that she probably had no idea how beautiful she was. She had straight, thick medium brownish-red hair that was pulled up in a ponytail. There were wisps of hair around her head that made Jason's groin tighten unexpectedly. He lost himself in her expressive brown eyes. They were the kind of eyes that spoke to his soul. He knew she had layers and was surprised by the thought that he might like that: enjoy getting to know her. Her skin tone was bright with a few freckles, and she looked to be just tall enough to reach his shoulder. She was dressed a little like a tomboy, in jeans, gym shoes, and a plain long sleeved t-shirt that hugged her curves. He could tell she had some strength in her upper body, and he found himself wishing he could see what was underneath that shirt. She looked just barely out of college. Definitely not his normal type.

Jason had had a thing for women that were older than him in the years past. Cougars some call them. They always knew what they were doing in bed and never bothered him for a commitment. He was always monogamous with the Cougar du Jour, not that he ever thought that they were going to be gone that quickly. He didn't expect them to be. Monogamy was just built into his character. It was who he was. His most recent cougar, Jennifer, had sated his needs until recently. She was a divorcee from a well-to-do suburb, and together they had fun. They'd meet at the same time twice a week at his condo. They'd share an hour of hot sex, and that had filled his needs until recently. He felt himself losing his desire for Jennifer. He felt like a robot when he entered her, and he thanked his lucky stars that she was none the wiser of his lack of interest because she usually was lost in her own passion. Recently, he'd started to think he was losing his mojo. It was depressing.

Reluctantly, he had admitted to himself that he wanted more. A wife. A family. Most of his friends were now married with kids. He'd spent the years building his business thinking that a family would weigh him down. He had a hard time admitting to himself that was what he now wanted, and he wondered if he'd waited too long. He wondered if all the good women out there were married. Hell, half the women he had as lovers were married. He'd thought of maybe trying a dating website but heard a lot of the people on there were not what they seemed to be. Frustrated, he'd put it to the back of his mind. Until now.

He didn't know what it was about this girl, but she took his breath away. He wished he had the time to approach her and find out who she was. He had a feeling it would be worth it, but business took precedence at the moment.

6

Kelsey had not been this angry since the day she'd found Zeke with Brittany. She wanted to find out who this real estate developer was and tell him to back off. The Dubickis were not going down without a fight. Mimi had asked her what was wrong, and Kelsey had just said she'd had a headache and wanted to go home. Mimi looked at her skeptically but decided not to push it when she saw the look in Kelsey's eyes.

As Kelsey stormed out of the mall with her fists rolled up into balls, she turned her head and saw a man staring at her from the coffee shop near the exit. She was surprised that amidst the sudden family chaos she would notice anyone, much less find a man attractive. All her thoughts of romance and the opposite sex had been dormant for the last year. She'd started to think maybe she'd be better off as a nun. Only she couldn't be in church that much or live in poverty. Then she saw these deep blue eyes that seemed to have a sparkle in them. It was almost as if they smiled at her and sensed her mood. Whoever he was, he was older, and she liked that.

The man with the beautiful eyes had short dark hair that looked like it had some styling product in it he could have only gotten from a salon. *That's the kind of hairstyle that he probably worked hard to make it look natural,* she thought with a bit of contempt. Still, his lips looked utterly kissable. She had always had a thing for full lips, and his seemed perfect. His skin was just golden enough to be suspect for this time of November in Minnesota. *He probably spray tans. Ugh.* He was almost too handsome for her and older than any guy she had dated. He was well-manicured and wearing a suit. Kelsey had always preferred the more working class kind of guy, and she was intrigued that she found this man attractive. She knew he was out of her league, but that didn't mean she wouldn't think about him and wonder.

7

That night, as Kelsey pulled her shiny red Hyundai Elantra coupe up to her family home, she was still literally seeing red. She'd been seething about the real estate developer responsible for this upheaval of their family business. She had to confess that the mysterious stranger in the coffee shop captured her thoughts, but her rage was still potent.

Kelsey walked into what was now the home of Adam and his family and greeted her sister-in-law, Stephanie. Stephanie was Scandinavian, like many families were in Minnesota. She was blonde-haired and blue-eyed and had the look of a girl that had been popular in high school. And she had been. Stephanie and Adam were married younger than they'd both expected when she'd found out she was pregnant with their first child. Adam said that having kids that soon had always been their intention, and Kelsey believed him. Her brother and sister-in-law seemed to be very much in love. Stephanie had just finished nursing little Jack. As she re-attached her nursing bra and put her top back down, she smiled and handed the little one to Kelsey. Kelsey loved her little nephew. She took a burp rag from his mommy and started to walk to the next room with Jack. There she found a pacing Adam.

"Where's Jesse?" she asked.

Adam shrugged and said, "Late as usual, I guess."

Adam started to bite his fingernail, a nervous habit he'd had since they were kids. They heard the front door and in walked Jesse with his blue hoodie over his head, looking as if he'd just been at the gym. He practically lived at the gym.

"Hey, Sis," Jesse said, leaning in to give her a kiss on the cheek. He gave little Jack a kiss and tousled his hair.

Jesse had eyes so dark they were almost black. He had an intensity to him that he brought into the ring when he fought. He was not that tall, 5' 8", but, what he lacked in height, he made up for in build. He was pure muscle. A lethal killing machine. He had started fighting in the underground fighting scene during high school which gave birth to his dream of being an MMA fighter. A dream he was very close to attaining.

"Hey, Adam. Stephanie. What's so important that I have to leave the gym?" Jesse said with a smile, winking at Stephanie.

Adam's jaw tensed, and he took a deep breath. Finally, he said, "As you know, there are real estate developers that want to build a high rise on the block Dubicki's is located. The butcher shop and Dubicki's are the last two places holding out. I received word this morning that the butcher shop is about to sign a deal. That leaves us. Now everyone else has sold but us, and the real estate company sees us as a roadblock. The amount of money that we were being offered was modest as first, but the aggression of Rourke Real Estate has grown. So has the amount they are offering us to sell."

Both Jesse and Kelsey had the Dubicki fire in their eyes. They looked at each other with the same look that said no one was going to take *their* legacy from them. Still, they let their eldest brother continue.

"Today, Jason Rourke offered me a million dollars to sell. In addition, he offered to retain the original bricks from the building so we could build anew. He let me know it was very important to him and that he would not stop until we reached an acceptable offer. I told him to leave and that we were never going to sell."

"I would have punched him," Jesse said.

Adam rolled his eyes.

"Yeah!" said Kelsey, agreeing with her brother Jesse.

"Listen, you two. This is why I own the bar. You both got the fiery temper of our mother. I am a little more even-tempered, like Dad, and you should be thankful. Physical violence does not solve anything."

"It's going to make me a living," said Jesse, under his breath.

Adam scowled at Jesse and continued. "So, I know that we are all on the same page as far as wanting to save the building our great-grandfather built. Still, it was too big of an amount of money for me not to tell you about it."

Jesse and Kelsey both folded their arms and shook their heads. "No!" they yelled at the same time.

"That's what I thought you'd say, but I had to let you know. We may not be able to fend this guy off forever," Adam replied.

Adam needed some aspirin. He could feel one mighty headache waiting to rear its ugly head. His siblings were going to need to cool down before logic could take over. In the meantime, he was hoping that terrible Jason Rourke didn't come knocking on his door again anytime soon. Or ever.

8

The next morning, Kelsey had to get up early. Every Thursday she had to go into the office to help Adam with inventory for the weekend and to go over the week's receipts and balance them with the books. She squinted against the sun that poured into her eyes as she entered the kitchen. It was a bright, sunny, fall day. She couldn't truly appreciate it, however, until she had her coffee. An hour later, she was in her car on the short drive to the bar. Every time she saw Dubicki's, her heart swelled with pride at the thought that it was her family that built it. That feeling alone reminded her that, no matter what amount the family was being offered, they could never sell or give up on their family business.

When she arrived at the bar, Kelsey greeted Adam and went to the back to do her thing. He was playing his favorite radio station, and she liked the music on the overhead. It helped her get in the zone and focus on the tedium of accounting. About 20 minutes into going through the receipts, Kelsey heard another male voice outside. It didn't sound like Jesse so she just shrugged her shoulders and figured it must be a vendor or someone Adam knew. As she went over the Monday night's receipts for the third time, she knew she was missing something. She needed more coffee, which was at the bar, so she finally got up to ask Adam about it. Blowing the wisps of hair that had fallen onto her forehead, Kelsey gathered her travel mug and the notebook with the balancing and headed towards the bar.

As she swung open the door that led to the bar, Kelsey looked up to see the source of the other male voice. She nearly dropped everything she was carrying. It was him. The guy from the coffee shop yesterday. The one who had the starring role in her fantasy last night, even if he didn't know it. She took in his dark hair, brooding eyes, and clean shave and wished she could lean over and smell his aftershave.

"Hi," said Kelsey.

"Kelsey, this is Jason Rourke, the owner of Rourke Real Estate," said Adam. "He's the real estate developer I told you guys about last night. Jason, this is my sister Kelsey."

"Nice to meet you, Kelsey," said Jason as he looked at her and smiled.

"Likewise, Mr. Rourke," said Kelsey.

She hoped the look she glared at him would kill him. No such luck. She quickly poured her coffee, collected her receipts, and stomped back to the office in the back of the bar. What a strange coincidence. First, she sees the first guy she has been attracted to in a year. Then, she finds out he's the enemy. It seemed like her luck wasn't getting any better after all.

9

Jason didn't know what had hit him. He had no idea the girl that he'd noticed the day before at the mall was a Dubicki. Her simple beauty had struck him, and he had thought about her ever since the moment he first saw her, which completely surprised him. He thought at first he was just thinking with his dick like whenever a hot chick walked by. When that occurred, as it often did, he would just take care of the itch with his current lover or, if all else failed, in the shower. Then he could move on and easily forget the thought of whatever woman had caught his eye. This was different. When she walked out from the back room today, his breath caught, and he felt like he'd been kicked in the gut. In a good way. She made his pulse race. Then he found out that she was the sister of the owner of the bar that he must buy to close this development deal. *Fantastic.*

He always kept his relationships casual. Since Michelle. Michelle had been his sweetheart. He had met her at his first real estate office. She was another young agent, and they had hit it off quickly. They got engaged and planned a wedding. Then she stood him up on their wedding day. His jaw tensed, as the very thought brought up an anger in him he had hoped he had long since buried. Looking back on it, their relationship had always been rocky. One minute they'd be making passionate love, and the next they'd be fighting. Every argument or disagreement was colorful, involving a lot of cursing and hand gestures. But, oh, when they had made up, they'd have the best make-up sex. Looking back, Jason realized he had just been young. He had almost married a woman that would have left him anyway, and he didn't believe in divorce. Now, Jason didn't believe in marriage. He believed in and supported everyone else's unions, but he had no interest in ever making that kind of commitment. He would never forget that would-be wedding day, how humiliated and broken-hearted he'd been. He had vowed that day never to give his heart to another woman. Being vulnerable was not for him.

Business is business. That was the way Jason Rourke looked at life. After the Michelle fiasco, he had spent the better part of his life building his business. He loved what he did, and it allowed him to stay focused on the future and not dwell in the past. While his friends had all been out partying, he had been closing real estate deals. They drank their money away, and he never saw a point to that. He'd earned a nice nest egg by the time he was 27. Now he owned several properties and had all the things a man could want. He had even been thinking about expanding the business to other cities, too. He could have anything he wanted, and what he wanted was to be the best at his business.

Jason had not realized that there had been anything missing in his life until the day he saw Kelsey Dubicki. She'd made him daydream about things he thought only the weak wanted: a wife, children, and the suburbs. He had shut that part of him out the day Michelle had left him at the altar. It had hardened his heart, and he had determined to keep all of his relationships casual and at arm's length since then. He had to shake this infatuation with Kelsey

Dubicki off because nothing was going to happen. No way, no how. He had to keep things in perspective and stay focused on the challenge at hand: buying Dubicki's.

Jason knew that even if he got casually involved with what was technically the opponent, he would lose focus. That was unacceptable. If he closed this deal, and he would, it would be the biggest real estate development deal of his career and one that would change the landscape of northeast Minneapolis. He could not let himself be distracted by the beautiful eyes of Kelsey Dubicki. She would challenge his business sense and his heart. He could just tell, and he didn't like it. It was time to give his current lover Jennifer a call so he could release some of the tension this was causing him. She would also help to steer his focus off of Kelsey Dubicki. He knew there was no way that any good could come from getting involved with Ms. Dubicki.

A few hours later, the doorbell to his penthouse rang. He heaved a sigh of relief when he saw Jennifer's pretty face and luscious curves. She had high cheek bones and beautiful red hair, and he'd always had a thing for redheads. That's what made him hot the first time he saw her. She was in her early forties and still had a hot body. She'd been a model when she was younger and still had the figure and beauty to prove it. She walked with erect posture and had an air of quiet confidence and sophistication to her. Today she had on a lace camisole that could be seen underneath her somewhat transparent top. She looked smoking hot.

"I thought you were ignoring me," Jennifer pouted.

He smiled as he grabbed her and swung her into his arms. He swung her tight little fanny up and sat her on the breakfast bar. He lowered his face to hers and gave her a kiss. She opened her mouth to him and all was forgotten.

"Are you wearing any panties underneath that skirt?"

"Why don't you find that out for yourself?" she asked in her husky bedroom voice.

27

Jason didn't say a word. His pants became crowded as his sex came to life. He enjoyed the slight discomfort, knowing that it was worthwhile as he dropped to his knees to solve the mystery of what was underneath that skirt. His hand skimmed up her smooth inner thighs. A soft moan escaped Jennifer's mouth. He touched the mound that he thought of as her rosebud through her panties. She was wet. He lowered his face between her thighs. All thoughts were lost except the pleasure at hand. It was going to be a fun afternoon.

10

Dubicki's bar was a brick stand-alone building in a part of the city where bars and similar buildings were common. There were two entrances to Dubicki's. One in the front and one on the side leading into the parking lot. When Adam had inherited the bar, it had been in need of a facelift. As an artist, Kelsey naturally had an eye for design and had talked her brothers into each giving a portion of their inheritance towards improving the interior of the bar. In the center of the main room was a long, rectangular bar. The bar itself was gorgeous. They had replaced the original bar with a custom-made mahogany one. It was flanked by green, granite-trim drink rails that gave it just enough flair to look rich but still remain practical. They had been able to help design all the shelving and space for inner work station items such as dishwashers and sinks inside the main bar. Overhead there were liquor cabinets that had been made to match the bar. Recessed lighting had been placed underneath each of the cabinets to add to the atmosphere. The bar stools matched the color of the décor, but they weren't foolish enough to have stools made of an expensive wood like they had used on the bar. With the amount of stools that were broken each month, they had to be able to order them and have an abundant supply if needed.

At the last minute in the design process, Kelsey had an epiphany of an idea. Many of the other existing bars had an old chalkboard next to the pull tab stand that boasted their menu or specials of the day. Kelsey wondered what it would be like to have an electronic, lit chalkboard with neon-glow markers. That idea evolved from having one for their daily specials into having a larger one that engulfed the wall next to the bar where the customers could write. It was always full, and they had to replace the special markers often. It made their patrons happy and gave them something to talk about, and it made the Dubicki clan smile to see what the customers would write. After a busy weekend night, the content wasn't always G-rated, but it was always erased for the next night.

Kelsey had a lot of work to do today. It was the day before Thanksgiving which was the busiest bar night of the year. All hands were on deck today, but there was still a lot to do before the doors opened at 2 p.m. It was early enough in the day to still have an underlying tone of liquor and olives in the air from last night's customers. The chef had just started cooking the specials for the night, and Kelsey found comfort in the smell of pierogis and Polish sausage as they cooked. A pierogi is a dumpling that is usually stuffed with something like cheese, and always found on a traditional Polish menu. There were different varieties of pierogis on their menu. Right now she savored the smell from the kitchen that reminded her of home. All of her life, part of her home had been at the bar and restaurant that was Dubicki's.

Dubicki's had three signature drinks. Signature drinks were the theme of many bars in this neighborhood. If there wasn't a signature drink, there was a signature theme. Since Zombies had become the rage in the last few years, there was even a zombie bar in town now. The other competitors had various beach or country-themed drinks.

One even had a drink line where all the drinks were named after a color. It was simple, and people loved it. Kelsey had been to the colored-drink bar several times when she had just turned 21, and she still shook her head in disgust thinking of the secret drinks that were really just vodka and different packaged kids' drink mixes dumped into a glass. She still couldn't get over that.

As a result of the themed drink craze in the city, she and Adam had created their own signature drink line: Dubicki's Tongue Series of drinks. To date, they had five of them: The Sharp Tongue, The Tongue & Cheek, The Loose Tongue, The Tongue Twister, and a shot called the Tongue Piercing. Each drink had a different blend of alcohol that made it taste like it sounded. The Tongue Twister was actually a crushed ice type of drink, and they even had a counter-sized frozen cocktail machine to support it. All of the recipes were highly classified, and every employee had to sign a non-disclosure agreement stating that they were never to disclose the recipe, regardless of whether or not they were employed by Dubicki's. All the themed drinks came with different garnishes on the glass, including the signature candy tongues that were made locally just for Dubicki's. As Kelsey oversaw the process of making all the pre-mix for the signature series of drinks, she got lost in thoughts of Jason Rourke. As much as she tried not to think of him, she could not get him out of her head. She knew that there was no way anything could happen, even if it was mutual, but that didn't stop her hormones from making her think about him. Of course, he was hot, but there was something in the way he looked at her that made her want to know him more.

Kelsey had been extremely angry when she realized that Jason was the person trying to take their bar. *What good would high rises do over here?* she thought. *This is one of the oldest neighborhoods in the city, and they're going to let them build overpriced condos here? What has this city become?* She had

31

stomped around for days listening to Rage Against the Machine on her iPod, along with all of her other angst-filled music she needed when something made her mad. Ever since her dad's death and Zeke's betrayal, she'd been building her rage song list longer and longer. She blasted the music and jammed along to the beat with the three other bartenders, preparing for big tips and lots of chaos, until all the prep work was complete.

At 1 p.m. the DJ came in and began setting up his equipment on the dance floor. They didn't have music like this all the time, but this was the beginning of the holiday season, their busy season, and it was worth every penny. The added bonus was that the staff would be able to jam right along with the DJ while he played his tunes and not have to stop to press play or change the song selection like they would on a normal night. Adam came out to give them encouragement about the night they had ahead of them. He told the staff they were all the best of the best which is why they worked at Dubicki's. He said to relax when the drunks got pushy with them and to just go with the flow. Tonight they had extra security to help with the crowds and the problems that could arise when the alcohol was flowing. They were stocked, they were staffed, and they were ready for the crowd. *Let the games begin.*

11

An afternoon of hot sex with Jennifer was enough to distract Jason temporarily, but then Kelsey came right back into his thoughts again. It was getting frustrating. Jason made himself some dinner, poured a glass of wine, and sat down to watch some UFC reruns. Sometimes he liked the amateur fights the best. Those were the fights that just contained raw fighting. These were the diamonds in the rough. As he was mid-way through his meal and looking down at his delicious plate of veal parmesan, angel hair pasta, and salad greens, he looked up in surprise as a familiar name came from the television.

"Now for the middleweight amateur division this evening, we have two well-matched contenders. From Omaha, Nebraska, we have Josh 'Thunder' Smith. His opponent is from Minneapolis, Minnesota... Jesse Dubicki."

Jason proceeded to watch what originally had seemed like a well-matched fight. It was over in two rounds with the Dubicki boy as the winner. He could see the resemblance to Kelsey and figured it had to be her younger brother. He wondered what Kelsey was up to tonight. Then he remembered that it was the night before

GABRIELLA SCOTT

Thanksgiving so she would undoubtedly be at the bar. He briefly thought of stopping by and then realized it would be mobbed. Add to that that, even if she did have a chance to talk to him, she probably wouldn't say anything without a string of expletives, and he decided to spare himself the frustrating experience. As he went to the fridge to see what he had for dessert, he realized that he'd forgotten to get his customary three bottles of wine that he got for every Rourke family Thanksgiving dinner. Thanksgiving with his parents always consisted of a large hybrid family. His parents had divorced when he was a teenager. At the time, he and his two siblings, Jenna and Jake, had all taken it really hard. It got even more difficult when his mom got remarried a year later. His mom and dad got along again, but the memory still stung when Jason thought of it.

Tomorrow there would be a whole house full of people. Jason's father, Tony, always brought Jason's paternal great-grandmother, Sissy. After the divorce, Dad had built a house and added an apartment for his grandmother. Although his dad dated a few times over the years, he had not remarried. Jason didn't think his father really ever found another woman he could love after being hurt by his wife leaving him. Jason understood. Jason's wife left him before she was his wife.

Jason's mom, Jerrilyn, always came with his stepdad, Billy. Jerrilyn and Billy had 16-year-old fraternal twins: Bridget and Ben. The twins favored the blonde hair his mother shared with her current husband. After Jason had gotten over the jealously of his mom leaving his dad and starting a new family, he had really taken a liking to his half-siblings.

Jason's 28-year-old sister Jenna also had their mother's hair paired with the classic good looks of their father. It made her gorgeous. Jenna's fiancé, Kyle, would be there, too. Kyle and Jenna had met in college and had been together in the years since. After two years being engaged, they'd finally set a wedding date, which was still two years away. Jason didn't know their reason for the wait, but he had learned the hard way that there's nothing wrong with taking things slowly.

Jason's younger brother Jake had never been on time for anything in his life, and no doubt he would be the last to arrive tomorrow. At 26, Jake was the baby of the Rourke siblings. The twins had their father's last name, Anderson. Jake was a handsome combination of his parents that was the opposite of Jenna. Jake had medium brown hair that was just long enough to look fashionable. Jason smiled as he thought about the men in his family liking their hair and the hair products that went with whatever look they were trying to achieve. Jake had brown eyes and also featured their mother's perfectly white teeth and dimples. Jake had the olive complexion of their half-Italian father, and ladies loved him. Jake developed video games for a living, and he was good at what he did, in demand, and paid well to do it. It was Jake's dream job and pretty much meant Jake was still a big kid at heart. Jason loved his little brother. They were so alike yet so different. Tomorrow, Jason would enjoy being with his family. There would be chaos, laughter and love. It was always good for his soul.

Jason got in his car to drive to the liquor store before it closed and got there just in time. As he was driving home, right before he crossed over the 3rd Street bridge back to downtown Minneapolis, he decided to take a right on Broadway. His car nearly drove itself to Dubicki's, as he'd been there so many times in the last few months. Now, as he neared Broadway and Marshall, he felt his palms start to sweat, and his breath quickened a bit. There was only one reason for that, and that was Kelsey Dubicki. A female had not made him feel like this in more years than he cared to count. Since then he had put his sole focus on business. In business, he always got what he wanted. He was used to getting what he wanted. What he wanted now was Kelsey

Dubicki.

As he made his way up to the steps of the bar, the chill of the November evening had him pulling up the collar of his jacket. One day he'd find a way to have a second home some place warm, like Florida. As the cold wind blew in his face, he pushed his way inside, past the unruly 20-somethings. He noticed that it was not just limited to youth in Dubicki's. This place had the feel of the old neighborhood, and there were plenty of people who looked like they had been here forever. They'd likely grown up here and raised families here. He was amazed that generations were there to enjoy a meal and a drink together the night before the holiday. He noticed that there was an array of traditional Polish food next to good old American food like potato skins and French fries on the menu. The menu consisted of whatever was scribbled on the modern version of a chalkboard. It was shiny and had fluorescent chalk that looked more like it might be a dry erase marker. One of the interesting things he noted was that next to the big menu chalkboard was a board that supplied chalk for customers to write on. Lots of obscenities were being written there this evening as people drank more and more. But there were also many expressions of love. He saw lots of initials, like BH + JA. Although it was totally out of character for him, he allowed himself to daydream about writing KD + JM on the board. He smiled. He felt like a completely hormonal teenage boy.

12

Kelsey could barely keep up with all the shouting of her customers. She couldn't help think that one of these days they should just get microphones and a PA speaker system. At that moment, anything would do, even a megaphone. She was afraid she was going to lose her voice by night's end. She and the rest of her three-person bartending crew had a good plan for tonight. They had set up a station in the center of the inner bar, like an island, for all the drinks that were popular tonight. Besides the various Tongue drinks, there were many other favorites, like the Irish Car Bomb, a shot of Irish Cream with Irish whiskey floated on top of it which is then dropped into a pint of Guinness stout. They made sure to leave a wide aisle around the island and, thankfully, had a couple great bar backs to help them replenish supplies and bus the dishes in and out.

As she methodically lined up six shot glasses in front of her to make six Tongue Piercing shots for a group of guys, she quickly brushed the hair out of her eyes. As she looked up, she noticed two eyes that were familiar in the distance. Jason Rourke. *What is that asshole doing here?* He was just standing there, staring at her like a zombie. Kelsey was mad. Anger gave her the energy she needed to make drinks fast and to shuffle through a long line of customers. What truly frustrated her was the fact that her body was betraying her. She felt a surge of pure lust for that man. Now she knew why they called it a primal instinct. As she looked up and wondered how she could get away from the bar for a minute, she noticed that Jason was getting in her line to order a drink. Kelsey looked down and didn't say a word.

13

Jason stood there for what felt like hours. When he looked at her, he felt like he was in a tunnel where the only people that existed were the two of them. There was no rationale for this feeling. He was mesmerized. Unless there was a business transaction involved, Jason was not the kind of guy to go into a bar alone, ever. Kelsey was just infecting his brain, his aura, his system. There was part of him that wanted it to go away so he could realign with his core, the core that focused on business and little else. Still, he couldn't resist whatever this feeling was. It was a delicious nuisance.

That is how he ended up standing in Dubicki's watching none other than the Princess Dubicki, Kelsey, slinging drinks all night on the night before Thanksgiving. If he had not been there, he would have been thinking about her, so he gave in to his desire. It took a while before he even gained the courage to get in line to get a drink from her. He had to spend a few moments taking in the beauty that was Kelsey. She had such a gorgeous skin tone, somehow still looking as if she'd been kissed by the sun despite daylight hours shortening as winter was upon them. She had such silky, beautiful reddish-brown hair pulled back all purposefully into a ponytail. He noticed she still had to control the flyaway hairs that escaped from the ponytail, and he found the very act of her frequently clearing her brow endearing. When she finally looked up at him, he could see the recognition in her big brown eyes. It gripped him down to his core. Jason could see fire in her eyes. She was furious at him for showing up, he knew. Yet, he suspected that the animation he saw in her gaze was composed of the same conflict he was feeling at the attraction they seemed to share.

As he stood in line waiting, trying to combat against the missteps of the other various drunks spilling their drinks on him, he still could not take his eyes off of her. When he finally got to the front of the line, he had no idea what to order. He just wanted to be near her. He found himself speechless for a moment when she snapped out a question.

"What'll ya have?"

He decided to try their signature drink, The Sharp Tongue, which seemed strangely apropos at the moment. She didn't say a word while she made it or when she handed him his drink. She was so efficient that he had a moment of regret that the exchange was over too fast. He could do nothing but make his way back through the crowd to the same spot where he'd stood previously, hoping to watch her for a little while longer. Normally he was confident in asking a woman out. He'd never been a praying man, yet he somehow felt that the obstacle of Kelsey being on the opposing side of a business transaction, and thus considering him an enemy, was a roadblock placed by God, if God did indeed exist. Jason could never turn away from a challenge, and neither God nor Kelsey Dubicki was exception to that.

14

Jason woke feeling refreshed on Black Friday, the day after Thanksgiving. He'd had a great time with his family the day before. As expected, his little brother Jake had been over an hour late, which they all loved to tease him about. They had purposely told Jake that dinner was earlier than they had planned, and he still managed to be late. Jason's mom had known something was up with Jason. She had asked Jason, point blank, who the girl was. Jason's eyes had grown big, and he had looked at her indignantly to show his surprise.

"Jason, I know you. You are my oldest child, and while the poker face you undoubtedly use in the majority of your business transactions works on other people, I am your mother. You can't fool me."

Jason's irritation had turned into a smile as he'd said, "Mom, it's complicated."

"Try me," she'd said.

Jason had spent an hour telling her about how he met Kelsey and how it was a complete conflict of interest because of his business goal to acquire her family's bar for his developers. He had even told his mom that somehow he could not shake his attraction to Kelsey and had gone to Dubicki's the night before just to stare at Kelsey. He had also told his mother that when he'd gotten the nerve to go get a drink from her, he was too nervous to say anything, just like a teenager.

Jerrilyn had smiled and said, "Oh, thank God. I was starting to think you'd hardened your heart after Michelle left you. What she did was terrible, but I was hoping you'd find love again. I always knew you had it in you, but I also knew you were stubborn enough not to go after it because you were so focused on business. I was starting to worry that you'd always be alone. I prayed, Jason. Prayed that my oldest son would find the woman of his dreams. I hope this is the answer to my prayers. I know things are difficult because her family is against you acquiring their business, but if it's meant to be, it will be. Now I might have to go in there and stalk her myself."

Then she had sat back and crossed her arms, satisfied.

"Mom, please don't do that. She probably already thinks I'm a stalker, and I don't need you adding to it."

They had joked about it, and his mother had said she'd make no promises not to stalk the girl but would try. *Hell, you'd know if Kelsey and I were dating,* Jason had thought, and he wasn't sure if he loved that thought or hated it. So, now here he was the day after Thanksgiving. Most of the rest of the city were either sleeping in or shopping all the early bird sales, but, to Jason, it was still a business day just like any other. He had mercy for the rest of his staff, letting them off for the day. Today was an opportunity to take care of loose ends and to enjoy the solace of being alone in his office.

At around 1:30 p.m., he had his first chance to breathe. He'd been immersed in papers all morning and highly productive as a result. He was a task-oriented man and easily able to lose himself in what he was doing. Not until now, while pondering what to tackle next, did he hear steps that sounded like someone coming down the hall. Perhaps he was not alone in his office building today.

Suddenly, there was a thunderous knock on his door. It made Jason jump in surprise, but he got up from the mound of papers scattered about his desk and curiously answered. The fact that it was a very angry-looking Kelsey Dubicki behind the door gave him even more of a start. God she was beautiful when she was angry. He tried not to smile.

"What the hell were you doing standing at my bar and staring at me for half the night?" demanded Kelsey.

"I decided to go out on Thanksgiving Eve along with the rest of the city. It's the busiest drinking night of the year. You should know that. Is there a problem?"

"Yeah, I'll tell you the problem. You! You've upset my entire family with wanting to destroy the place that my family built. There's no amount of money that can buy us, don't you know that by now! Further, why did you have to stand there near me? You know that Adam is the one you should be talking to about this."

"You're a feisty girl, aren't you?" Jason said, trying not to chuckle. His eyes sparkled with laughter as he looked at her. He fought the urge to reach out and touch her face or brush the hair out of her eyes.

"For your information," Jason continued, "I was at Dubicki's because I wanted to see how the business ran. Your brother keeps trying to talk me into his keeping it. While that option is really not on the table, I figured I would do my duty and check it out."

"Then why did you stand there staring at me all night? It was unnerving." Kelsey looked frustrated and settled her eyes to the side. She couldn't look at him, yet she didn't want to look away.

"Kelsey, what is unnerving to me is how I've been taken with you since I first laid eyes on you. I'm not a man who loses focus from business. Ever. Yet, somehow I can't stop thinking about you. I know very well that we are on opposite sides of this business transaction. That you consider me enemy number one. I get that."

Kelsey folded her arms across her chest and signed with impatience. Her look told him to continue.

"I've never been able to take no for an answer. I like a challenge. That's why I haven't left you and your brother alone. I intend to have that block for development purposes. Whatever it takes. You, Kelsey, are no exception to my not being able to resist a challenge."

Jason quickly closed the gap between the two of them and lowered his lips to hers. He put his arms against the wall on each side of her, and he kissed her. She fought him at first but quickly became pliant within his arms. She wrapped her arms around his neck and let out a sigh. She offered him her tongue, and he opened his mouth to accept it. She tasted so good it was intoxicating. He kissed her gently at first, and then his urgency increased. His hand slowly crept down her neck. She moaned and lifted her chest to him. Jason couldn't resist but to feel her breasts as his hands glided over her clothes. He thought he'd explode right there just from touching her, tasting her, breathing her in.

Kelsey was the first one to regain her senses and pull away from the experience they were about to create if they continued. She quickly buttoned up her coat and curtly said, "I better go."

He smiled and nodded his acknowledgement as he remorsefully watched her walk away. In a daze, Kelsey walked out of the skyscraper that housed Rourke Real Estate. *What just happened?* She went there to confront Jason Rourke, not make out with him! She decided that since she was downtown and didn't have to be to work for a few hours that she'd take the opportunity to go to Macy's department store. They had an amazing eighth floor holiday display. As a child, the store had been Dayton's before being bought by Macy's, and every year since she could remember the eighth floor auditorium had been decorated in a holiday theme, such as *A Christmas Carol* or *The Grinch*. Life-like dramatizations made for both children and adults alike showed various scenes as you made your way through the display. At the end, you were able to buy souvenirs, cookies, cocoa, and candies. Children could even get their picture taken with Santa.

Kelsey figured it would be crowded today because of the kick-off to the holiday season, but she really needed the distraction that would take her back to the innocence of childhood for a while. She had to wait in line for an hour but finally made her way through to the auditorium. This year it was a treat because it was a compilation of scenes from various years of displays since the tradition had started in 1963. In one window was *Cinderella*. The next had *The Grinch*. The next had *Snow White*. Kelsey felt the tears in her eyes as she saw familiar scenes she remembered going through with her family as her child. Where did time go? She wished she would have known to savor those moments all the more because she and her brothers wouldn't have their mom and dad for nearly long enough.

She smiled at all the parents and little children. A couple of crying babies brought her back to the present moment. All the memories of the past built her resolve to find a way to keep Dubicki's intact and away from Rourke Real Estate. She just didn't know how she was going to keep herself away from Jason Rourke in the process. After that kiss today, Kelsey found it difficult to control her feelings for him. She was attracted to him. That was sure. She also felt a depth that went beyond that. She'd liked that he called her feisty, and he was right. She just didn't know how she'd toe the line with her brothers and deal with the fact that Jason Rourke was the enemy of the Dubicki family. She pushed that issue to the back of her mind and decided she had better get back to her apartment so she could change clothes and get to work.

15

Kelsey hung her coat in the back office at Dubicki's and pulled her hair into a ponytail. As she walked into the front where the bar was, Adam came back up from checking the stock downstairs.

"Did you hear that Jason Rourke was in here on Wednesday night?" Adam asked.

"Uh, yeah. It was annoying. He walked in here and stood at the back of the bar near the chalkboards and just stared. It took him about a half-hour before he even came up to buy a drink."

Kelsey's mind quickly went to the passionate kiss she had shared with Jason Rourke that afternoon, and she hoped her face didn't flush and betray her to Adam.

"He talked to you?" said Adam.

"Only to order his drink," Kelsey said as she looked down and bit back a smile. She should have taken acting classes instead of art classes. They'd sure come in handy right about now.

"Well, come Monday I am going to call his office to find out what he's up to. If he wants to make another offer, he better make it, but I will not tolerate him here intimidating us," Adam said crossly.

"I went to his office this morning and gave him a piece of my mind. It made me mad the way he stood there all night," Kelsey admitted.

"Kelsey, what the hell were you thinking? You shouldn't be doing that without consulting me first. I talk on behalf of our family, is that understood?"

Kelsey tensed her jaw as she often did when she was angry. She nodded in agreement and decided it was not the time to show Adam her cards just yet. She and Jason had only kissed. She had a feeling tonight would be nearly as busy as Wednesday night was because it was still Thanksgiving weekend. That meant lots of out-of-town family members were still in town. Whether that made them happy or stressed out, one thing was always guaranteed: her customers always wanted to get away from it all. That usually also meant that they wanted to drink copious amounts of alcohol. Dziadek was smart when he opened this business. Whether people were happy or sad, or economic times were good or bad, liquor was always in demand.

As she set up her station for the night, an activity that was always cathartic to her, she thought of the things that Jason Rourke said. That he'd have her. That he'd have this bar. She wasn't too sure about that, but she knew she would not easily forget that kiss or the way she felt when he touched her. She might not have been ready to show the cards of what happened that afternoon to her brothers, but neither was she ready to show her hand to Jason Rourke yet, either.

16

The next day, Kelsey left her apartment for work. As she walked downstairs, she spotted Jason Rourke down the walk, standing near his car and watching her. He stood there looking confident. He was dressed in a suit and a winter overcoat that made him look like the businessman that he was. His dark hair looked well-coiffed as usual, and she bet he smelled delicious. His very presence exuded power. A power she'd like to feel when used to her benefit in bed. She bit her lower lip lightly as naughty thoughts ran through her head. As she took in the sight of him, her heart jumped, and she felt the butterflies that were now becoming familiar to her when she was near him. It was unnerving. And intoxicating. She gingerly walked toward him. He had an intensity to his eyes, and she liked that about him. It kind of scared her, but she found it hard to resist. *Damn, he looks sexy.*

"Hi," he said

"Hi, yourself," Kelsey said. "What brings you here?"

"You. I figured I'd better come and speak to you at your home because the bar is dangerous territory for us meeting. It may bring up questions with your family that you're not ready to answer."

"Agreed."

"But if you think that I am going to leave you alone after that kiss, I'm sorry," Jason told her. "I won't leave you alone unless you ask me to. I am here to ask you if you would go on a date with me."

Somehow, this all made Jason feel like a schoolboy. He didn't like feeling like a teenager again, but he knew the train had already left the station, so to speak. The beauty of Kelsey's smile made it all worthwhile. Kelsey sighed. She couldn't contain the slow smile that spread across her face as she blushed.

"I suppose I'd like that," Kelsey admitted. "It has to be our secret, though. I don't know what my brothers would say, but I don't think it would be good."

"Agreed," Jason concurred. "So, do you ever get a night off from the bar?"

"Tuesdays and Thursdays are my days off."

"Okay, so how about Tuesday night I pick you up at about 6:30?"

"It's a date," said Kelsey.

Jason closed the space between them and lowered his face to hers. He paused for a moment. She inhaled his scent and felt his warm breath on her face. It stirred her desire for him. He looked down at her as his eyes grew intensely dark.

"Do you want me to kiss you?" he whispered.

He lowered his lips close to hers and gently brushed over her lips with a feather-light touch. Kelsey quietly moaned.

"Is that a yes?" he asked quietly.

She could only nod her consent.

He again lowered his lips down to her and gently licked her bottom lip with the tip of his tongue. She shivered in anticipation. He lifted his finger up to her lip, and gently brushed her chin as his lips found hers. His tongue was hungry and impatient, and she anxiously parted her lips for him. He hungrily ingested her taste, her scent. He couldn't get enough of her. He forced himself to step away as he felt his erection through his pants. His saving grace was his overcoat, or she would surely have felt the depth of his sexual attraction to her. He gently wiped his thumb over her lip, and then he kissed her on the check.

"I better let you get to work," Jason said softly. "I'm looking forward to our date."

Kelsey couldn't find her words after that kiss. She smiled and nodded as he got into his car and drove away. She hoped she'd be able to focus on work and not walk into walls tonight. She couldn't control the butterflies she had, but when she thought of what her brothers might say, it quite effectively brought her back down to earth. She got into her car, put on her sunglasses, and decided to blast the music loud. If singing to the top of her lungs didn't help her get her mind off of all of this, she was in trouble.

17

Kelsey couldn't wait to tell Mimi that she had a date. The tricky part would be how and what to tell Mimi, but Kelsey needed Mimi's advice on what to wear, among other things. It had been a long time since Kelsey had been on a date. Zeke and Kelsey had just kind of fallen into their relationship. She wasn't sure if you could call Chinese food and a DVD at home or playing darts and shooting pool with friends a date. It was funny that she'd never realized until now that she had yet to have a proper date with anyone.

"Hello?" Mimi answered on the first ring

"Hi! Do you have time to hang out, soon? I need a new outfit. I kind of have a date," Kelsey said excitedly.

"WHAAATTT! Give me the dish – NOW!"

"Well, it's just someone I happened to meet at the bar."

"Kelsey, you should know better than to get involved with the drunks at the bar. I hope it wasn't some guy with a drunken slur at the end of the night."

"Uh, thanks. You could give me a little more credit than that. Yes, I met him at the bar, but we were both sober. And it was over a business transaction of sorts."

"Kelsey, what are you not telling me?"

"Well, I don't know how to say this, and you have to promise not to tell Adam or Jesse. It's the owner of the real estate firm that wants to buy the bar."

"You have GOT to be fucking kidding me. What? Do you have a death wish? Because either this guy is going to be the death of you or your brothers will kill you. Couldn't you at least wait until the deal with the bar is done or over or something?"

"I know, Mimi, but then he kissed me."

"What? When? How was it?"

"I'll tell you all about it when you meet me at the mall in two hours. Can you handle that?"

Mimi sighed and agreed to the meeting. Shopping was not a dilemma for her. Having to wait for details from her best friend, on the other hand, was going to drive her nuts.

After all was said and done, they had a really fun afternoon. Even though Mimi did some scolding of what her brothers would do to Jason if they found out, Mimi was as excited for Kelsey as any good girlfriend would be. They picked out a couple of outfits; one Mimi liked, and one more Kelsey's style. After all the extra accessories and shoes, Kelsey felt nearly ready for her date.

18

Jason decided to dress down a little for his date. He spent the majority of his time in suits and ties. He also knew that Kelsey seemed a little more down to earth, so he didn't want to make her feel uncomfortable. He still couldn't get over the feelings he was having for her. He had never allowed himself to be overcome with emotion about a girl, not really even Michelle. When he was younger, he had watched all of his hormonal friends lose control over girls. He never understood it. It wasn't that he hadn't appreciated girls; it was just that he liked to remain in control of things. Even his relationship with Michelle somehow kept him from having the feelings of insanity that he associated with relationships. Maybe that was why they had failed.

Still, Jason did enjoy the company of a woman. Often. He had always had a healthy libido and knew how to find the woman that would have the fewest strings attached to satisfy his physical needs. For the last few years, that system had worked for him quite effectively. Then he met Kelsey Dubicki.

It was a good thing that in the beginning of his attempted negotiations he'd only talked to her eldest brother Adam. If Jason had met Kelsey that early on, it would have thrown off his business savvy. Until he'd met Kelsey a couple of weeks ago, he'd never known what the heck all the guys were thinking when they allowed themselves to be completely consumed by the opposite sex. There was something about her for which there were no words. Now he understood the old wives' tale that said, "You just know when you know." He didn't have to be a betting man to know that his days of holding the upper hand in his dating relationships were numbered. The enchantment that he was starting to feel clouded his ability to think about how bad this relationship could devastate his real estate development deal. He'd never felt this way before, so he was just going to go with the flow and follow his heart. He only hoped he didn't end up bankrupt or heartbroken because he allowed his heart to rule his brain.

19

Kelsey had changed her shirt five times. Her bed was an array of discarded clothing choices, but her present emotional state took precedence over the mess that was her room right now. The shirt Mimi had chosen for her seemed a little too provocative. It had seemed like a good idea at the time. Now the thought of showing a little cleavage felt a little more suggestive (and slutty) than she wanted to feel right now. Kelsey settled on a soft yellow V-neck sweater. It still highlighted her bust line without overdoing it. She seldom thought of herself as a clothes horse. Her fashion choices were usually classic and straight forward: solid colors, practical fabrics, and jeans or shorts. Tonight she decided on black skinny jeans with a new pair of black patent leather flats that Mimi had helped her pick out. Mimi had argued with her over leaving her hair down, and that was the one concession that Kelsey stuck to this evening. Her hair hung just below her shoulders in soft waves, and she had to admit she liked looking just a little more feminine for a change. She'd never had a reason to before, nor at least in a long time had there been a reason.

At 6:29 p.m. her doorbell rang. *He's prompt.* She liked that quality in a man. She answered the door and tried not to actually gasp as she saw the gorgeous sight that was Jason Rourke. He wore a purple, long-sleeved, button-down shirt that hung outside of his jeans. The jeans were the pique of fashion on men, complete with a little bling on the back pockets. They fit his body perfectly. Kelsey had a feeling he'd purposely dressed down, yet he still looked as polished as always. He was clean shaven, and she loved that his hair was so dark that he looked like he could spring a five o'clock shadow at any time. It would still be sexy if he did. He smelled of a hint of aftershave, and she liked that he didn't overdo it. Kelsey couldn't help but study every inch of him. She hadn't realized that she'd missed having a man around until the kiss the other day.

"You're looking at me very closely, Miss Dubicki. If I didn't know any better, I'd say you have the hots for me," Jason said with a smile.

Kelsey could feel her face flush. The only time her face ever betrayed her was when she was embarrassed. She couldn't control the fact that she flushed from her head to her neck to her chest. She apologetically lowered her gaze away from him.

"You know I didn't mind that you looked at me like that. In fact, I liked it. I must say, you look beautiful tonight, Kelsey," Jason told her as he handed her some roses he'd had behind his back. "These are for you."

Pink roses! Kelsey didn't know that there were guys that actually did nice things like that. She thought that only happened in the movies.

"Thank you," Kelsey said, trying to find words. This guy made her tongue-tied. She made a note to herself to consider adding a drink with that name to the signature drink selection at the bar. *Tongue Tied. I can't believe we never thought of that one before.*

"Earth to Kelsey. Where'd you go on me?" Jason interrupted her rushing thoughts.

Kelsey shook her head as she popped back into reality.

"Oh, I'm sorry. What were you saying?" Kelsey asked.

"Well, I wanted to say this…."

Jason leaned down and kissed her. The kiss was sensual, just like the others had been, and it took them a few minutes to come up for air.

"I have reservations for a great new restaurant on Eat Street for us at 7:15. We'd better get going" Jason said, and Kelsey nodded in agreement. Eat Street was a well-known area in the city celebrated for award-winning restaurants from many ethnicities that continued for blocks.

"Sounds great! I'll get my coat," Kelsey said.

"Here, Kelsey, let me help you get your coat on," Jason offered.

Kelsey tried not to look at him like he was from outer space. It wasn't her fault she'd never had a guy treat her like a lady before. She decided to go with the flow and just enjoy being spoiled by a man. He wrapped her coat around her in a way that made her feel treasured. She could get used to this.

20

As they were seated in the restaurant, Kelsey's appreciation of her date grew. The atmosphere in the place was perfect for a first date. It was warm and upscale but not too over-the-top. She'd been afraid he'd take her to a restaurant out of her league, but this place felt like he had put some thought into who she really was. Just like any woman, she liked a nice restaurant, but she was down-to-earth enough to not want to sit down with a pretentious crowd and a menu too extravagant for her tastes.

"So, do you like what you see, Kelsey?"

Kelsey's face flushed when he said that.

"No, I don't mean me," Jason chuckled. "The restaurant?"

"Oh! I was just thinking what a nice place this is. It's perfect."

"I'm glad you like it."

They were seated at a table near the back of the restaurant near a crackling fireplace. Since they were at a table with four chairs, Jason took the seat right next to her after Kelsey chose where she'd sit.

The server came and took their order. Jason ordered a bottle of Pinot Noir from Chile for them to share.

Good choice, thought Kelsey

"So, Kelsey, tell me about yourself. It's obvious that your family is from northeast Minneapolis, but what was your life like before I met you?"

Kelsey told Jason stories of her parents and her brothers, and Jason laughed at the stories that in some ways reminded him of his own family. She got emotional when she spoke of the death of her parents, and even more emotional at the thought that they might lose the family business. She told him that, in some ways, it was all she had left of her parents

"Kelsey, I'm sorry. I've spent my whole life building my business, and not only do I think I do that well, but I'm competitive. I wanted to be the best real estate business in the city, and I'm now in the top three. I never saw the personal aspects of the business transaction because, to me, business is business. Then I met you. Don't think I haven't considered that my seeing you might somehow affect this deal for better or worse."

Kelsey looked down and thought for a moment before she spoke. "It hadn't occurred to me until just now that it might be difficult for you, too. It's an emotional situation for my family. It's all my brothers, and I have left of the business that my grandfather built. I will do my best not to talk about this too much because I realize that there are two sides of the situation, Jason."

Jason continued, "I'm trying my best to compartmentalize my emotions in a somewhat complicated situation. I will say this, though. I'm sorry for the grief that this has been causing you and your family. I've been under pressure to meet my goals. I have respect for a family that will not compromise."

"Thank you, Jason, it's nice to hear that you respect our family. It's still a difficult situation for all of us. I don't know what I will do if my brothers find out we've been out," said Kelsey

"The one thing I never expected in the process of this

GABRIELLA SCOTT

business deal was to meet a woman that made me think
outside the box of the deal. That's never happened to me
before. Ever. Normally, I would just move on and never
ask anyone out, even if I wanted to, if business were
involved. But I haven't been able to get you out of my
mind. I was instantly drawn to you. You intrigue me. I
don't know what will come of this, but I want to get to
know you if you'll let me."

"I don't know what to say to that, Jason."

"Say that you'll let me get to know you, Kelsey."

"Well, I'm here, aren't I?" she said and smiled, and he
noticed that she had one dimple when she did.

"So, tell me a little more about you and your
background, Jason."

Jason spent the next 20 minutes filling her in on his big
extended family. Kelsey had a hard time with all the J
names and said she was thankful that her siblings' names
all started with different letters. Jason entertained her with
stories of how his brother and sister used to get in trouble.
One day, when their parents were gone, they all decided to
sled down the stairs.

"Sled!" she exclaimed, as he nodded and continued.

"The stairs to the basement that we used went down,
and there was a wall at the base of them. I was young and
didn't take into account that I was a little bit tall to be
sledding in the family home. Never mind that it was
dangerous. I made my run down the stairs on my belly,
and my head crashed through the paneled wall at the foot
of the stairs."

They both laughed until they cried as he told her that
story and many more of the antics of the Rourke siblings.
She told him some stories about her siblings, but they
laughed the hardest at how he had busted through the wall
with his head. Thankfully, the wall had been panel, so the
wall bore more damage than Jason did at the time. He still
got grounded for two weeks, and Kelsey and he laughed
some more.

Jason also told Kelsey all about how his grandmother, Sissy, his dad's mom, was from the south of Italy. Jason was half-Irish and half-Italian, and he said it gave him more depth and character. His grandmother Sissy believed that she was clairvoyant and would often say she had visions. He laughed when he told Kelsey that Sissy said that every once in a while she tried to cast a spell.

"Her spells never worked," Jason laughed. "It still effectively scared her card-playing club into letting her win almost every time. She made a killing for a while until they all decided to bet candy. That probably didn't happen until my grandmother had cleaned all the other old ladies out of their life savings."

"She sounds like a hoot!" Kelsey said and laughed even more.

"She is. I really love her. Maybe sometime you could meet her."

"I don't know, she might try to put a spell on me. I'm afraid of what might happen."

Kelsey blushed and looked down. She loved teasing him. She loved the conversation they were having. He wanted her to meet his family. She wasn't sure if she was ready for that. Yet. She nipped at her bottom lip as she contemplated that. Jason put his arm over the back of her chair. He leaned in, and she felt his warm breath on her cheek.

"Do you have any idea how sexy you look right now? When you bit your lip, it made me squirm a little," he said as he lowered his lips to hers.

Kelsey lifted his face to him. They shared a sweet and somewhat chaste kiss. She liked that he wasn't overly into public displays of affection. Kelsey already felt herself losing control sexually when she was near him, and she certainly didn't want that happening in public. Jason sighed with her sweetness on his lips as he pulled away from their kiss. This woman was driving him nuts. In a good way. He felt himself falling for her a little more each moment. This was going to be Heaven, or this was going to be Hell. Something told him that there was no in between.

21

After dinner, Jason had arranged a horse-drawn carriage ride. Luckily, the weather was cooperating that night. You never knew in Minnesota, but it was as if there were angels paving the way for them on their first date. Not that Jason would ever admit that there was any such thing as angels. The carriage took them all along the streets of the city. They were even able to see an outdoor ice rink, and, since it was a nice night, there were lots of people out skating. Kelsey rested her head on Jason's shoulder. He opened his arms and brought her to his chest. Somehow, with the two of them, even silence was comfortable, and he heard her sigh with contentment echoing the way he now felt, too. He gently stroked her back as they rode along.

They had such easy conversation at dinner, and Jason found that Kelsey had a sense of humor that complimented his. She was smart and sarcastic, and he liked that. He'd told her all about his family, how his parents had been divorced when he was 13 and how he had a stepdad that he liked and two half-siblings as a result of his mother's second marriage. He had grown up in the southwest suburbs of Minneapolis, which Kelsey teased that it explained his flair for the excessive. Jason told her he would take that as a compliment, and he teased that Kelsey was an equally snooty city kid who looked down on kids from the suburbs. They both had a good laugh and learned they liked to tease each other.

Now, as their carriage ride was turning back around towards their starting point, they both sighed knowing that this night would soon be over. Neither of them wanted the end to come so soon. They were markedly silent as Jason drove Kelsey home. He reached over and grabbed her hand, and she let him. She looked at him and smiled.

"Thank you for tonight," she said.

"It is you who I should thank, Kelsey. Thank you for taking the risk to go out with me."

When they got to Kelsey's apartment, Jason walked her up to her door. He leaned in and asked with his eyes if she wanted a kiss. She was starting to feel his kisses were a drug and anxiously reached up to kiss him. When his lips touched hers, it took her breath away, just like it did each time they kissed. She opened her mouth and gently offered her tongue to him. He responded hungrily. They lost themselves for a few moments, and Jason finally pulled away. He looked at her for a few moments as if he were trying to see into her soul. She smiled at him and reached her hand up to caress his cheek. He leaned into her hand and put his hand on hers.

"Can I call you?" Jason asked.

Kelsey nodded and smiled. She liked that idea but shook her head in disbelief as Jason left. Kelsey had a feeling that her life was about to change. She sighed as she walked into her apartment. She just didn't want to get her hopes up too high. All hell could break lose when her brothers found out. Jason and Kelsey would not be able to keep this relationship a secret if things kept moving forward. She could somehow see herself spending forever with this man. She just wasn't sure what that meant for the future of Dubicki's.

22

Two evenings later, Jason came back for a second date. This one featured Chinese takeout and a movie. Jason even brought Kelsey's favorite local beer, appropriately called *Nordeast*. The neighborhood she lived in was often referred to as Nordeast because of the way it was pronounced by the Polish, Ukrainian and other primarily Eastern European immigrants that established and were still in the neighborhood today. She may have been a mixologist of a bartender at work, but she was a good, old-fashioned beer-lover at heart.

They continued to find out more about each other. It seemed uncanny how much they had in common for two people so different. They were quickly falling into a familiar rhythm with each other. They loved to debate anything and everything. Most recently they'd been debating Jason's love of opera. Kelsey could not find anything desirable about opera and was not afraid to tell Jason that. Jason was determined to take Kelsey to an opera and change her mind.

Today they were debating the meat raffle. The pubs on this side of town often featured meat raffles. A meat raffle was a tradition in pubs that typically featured a nice cut of meat supplied by a local butcher. You could win if you bought a ticket; tickets were typically one dollar. Jason could not seem to understand the importance of a meat raffle because so many people were vegetarians now, but that was just the way that things were done here in this neighborhood steeped in tradition. When Kelsey told Jason that bar crawls were becoming a trend in the neighborhood, he looked at her in disbelief.

"You're kidding, right?" he questioned.

"People seem to love to gather and walk from bar to bar drinking along the way. Northeast Minneapolis is a good area to do so because of all the drink-themed bars." Kelsey explained. "It started slowly, but then caught on. People now organize bar crawls, and some of the bars support drink specials just for that particular event. The crowds have gotten bigger and bigger. It's nuts if you're behind the bar, and fun if you're in front of it. I've been on both sides of the bar during a good bar crawl. You should try it sometime."

"Uh, yeah, I don't know," Jason said, shaking his head and smiling.

Jason could think of more than a few of his friends that still loved to go out drinking that would probably love a pub crawl. He realized they had probably already been to a bar crawl, or three, and resolved to ask them about it.

"I used to have one group that always came through Dubicki's before the trend exploded and the groups became too large to keep track of," Kelsey told him. "There was one girl that lived in the neighborhood and told me that there was a strategy to it all. Eat a good meal. Pace yourself. Don't drink at every bar. And if all else fails, when you get so drunk you fall down, it's time to go home."

They both laughed. They realized that they both loved spicy food, which was a good thing since the majority of the dishes that Jason brought that night were spicy. His favorite sport was baseball. Hers was a tie between hockey and football. Kelsey said she could watch any sport with a ball as long as it was not a golf ball. Jason was slightly deflated at that since he loved golf, but at least he could still enjoy golf with his clients. He was just happy that she liked sports at all. *Thank goodness she was raised with brothers,* he thought.

23

They cuddled as they watched the movie. Jason was polite enough to wait until the credits were rolling to lift her head to his and kiss her beyond a peck on the lips. He was surprised at how hungry Kelsey seemed to be for him, and he liked it. They made out for a while, and when Jason finally took a moment to come up for air he asked, "Kelsey, do you want more than this?"

She bit her lip and nodded, encouraging him to explore her body more. Jason lightly kissed her again and began to touch her face and neck while he kissed her. He lowered his lips to her neck and kissed a trail to her ear, where he nibbled and licked her earlobe. She let out a throaty moan, and he shivered with anticipation. He gently ran his hand up her arm to her collarbone. He lightly touched her chin and trailed his finger down the center of her chest. Once he got to her cleavage, he stopped and looked at her. He could see the lust in her eyes which encouraged him to continue. He gently skimmed the outline of the camisole showing beneath her button-down shirt. As he gently brushed his thumbs up against her nipple, she moaned. He brushed his hand underneath her breasts. He felt his cock twitch, and his jeans were feeling more constricting with each moment. Still, he had to take it slow with her. He loved the little sounds she was making and wanted to savor each moment.

Jason started to slowly unbutton her shirt. He heard her breath quicken with impatience. He looked up at her and smiled. He gave her lips a quick kiss and then returned his focus to where he had left her blouse open. She still had her camisole on, and he wanted to have fun a little bit more. He went to her shoulder and moved the right strap just off her shoulder. He did the same with her left. Her eyes grew big and again he saw impatience, but he knew that good things were worth waiting for.

He trailed kisses from her neck down to the top of the camisole beneath her shirt. He gently pulled the fabric over her right breast. He lightly moaned in appreciation as he saw her beautiful breasts for the first time. They seemed swollen just for him. He took his time loving each one of them. Gently kissing and licking each of them, caressing one as he licked the other. Kelsey moaned and started to buck her hips. He lifted his mouth to hers and kissed her for a few moments. He whispered to her that she must be patient.

"Do you like this, Kelsey?"

Kelsey gave a breathy moan in response. He returned to her beautiful breasts to suckle each one a bit more before continuing on. He trailed kisses down to her navel before asking her again if she wanted him to continue. She moaned and bucked her hips.

"Yes!" she cried.

He started to unbutton her jeans. Every time he wondered if he was going too fast, she responded with a move or moan of encouragement. Slowly, he pulled off her jeans. She had on pink, silky panties that were soaked in the center. *Oh dear God*, Jason thought, not knowing if he was going to make it. He took a moment just to take her in, unbuttoning his shirt while doing so. He removed his shirt, and then unbuttoned the top button of his jeans.

Kelsey looked at him with the most beautiful brown eyes. The eyes that said she wanted to see him, wanted this. He put his hand to his zipper.

"Do you want me to take my pants off?"

She nodded in a shy but anxious way. Slowly, he eased his zipper down and then slid his jeans down his body a little bit at a time. When he was out of most of his clothes, he exposed a muscular physique, and Kelsey smiled in appreciation. All that he was left in were his gray boxer briefs that exposed his erection. Kelsey looked down at him with appreciation and impatience, and he focused his attention back on her legs and the gorgeous wet spot in her panties. He slowly kissed up each inch of her leg from her feet until he got to her inner thighs. She spread her legs further open for him and bucked her hips with impatience. Jason took his time kissing each one of her inner thighs. He was careful not to remove her panties. He liked to tease her a bit and feel her squirm. He touched the outside of the panties with his lips, and, just as he got above the wet spot, he lifted his head and breathed hot air onto her there.

"Jason, what are you doing to me?"

"Patience, love."

Kelsey sighed and put her hands on the tops of her panties as if to take them down. Jason responded by placing his hands on top of hers to keep them in place. She pouted; he thought it was darling. He went back to breathing all over the outside of her panties and nuzzling her there with his face. Kelsey felt like it would be the death of her. Just then, Jason gently took one side of the crotch of her panties and slid it to the side. He gently put his finger on her, and she responded again by lifting her hips. He decided it was time to relieve her, but not before he had a little fun.

Jason gently let his fingers fondle her clit, and it was so wet for him that his body's response was to leave his own wet spot on his boxers in anticipation. He didn't want her to come yet, so he forced himself to stop. She whimpered. He responded by shimmying the panties down off of her and lowering his head into her warmth. He slowly tasted and licked his way all over her sweet mound. He loved the taste of her, and she bucked impatiently at the feel of his tongue on her. He still wanted to take his time exploring her folds, and it was not until he was satisfied that he focused on truly pleasing her. He finally focused on her swollen clit and touched the tip of his tongue to her, first slowly and then gradually faster. She responded by grabbing a fist of his hair and yelled his name as her body erupted with spasms that said she had come. Jason continued to lick her gently, and she sighed in appreciation with each of her body's residual spasms. He gently lifted his head.

"You tasted so good, Kelsey. Did you like that?"

She nodded. He found it so hot that she was still gently touching herself, rubbing her hands over her breasts and even letting her fingers linger into her pussy as if she didn't mind him watching.

"You're relaxed, and I like that," he said

"I forgot how good sex can be. Now I'm thinking it's never been this good." She bit down on her lip and smiled at him.

"The night is still young, Kels, if you want more."

"Of course, I want more," she said, smiling.

Jason was relieved and took his time taking his own boxers down. He saw her eyes get big as she took in his size, and he figured that was partly due to her inexperience. He liked that. She looked down at his glistening cock with sheer lust in her eyes.

"Do you want me inside of you, Kelsey?"

Again, she moaned and nodded.

"Do you have any condoms?" he said.

She rolled over, produced one from near her bed, and tossed it to him. He quickly covered himself and began to kiss her. He wanted this to be nice and slow. Slowly he

71

kissed her mouth, trailed his tongue to her ears and down her breasts. As he raised his body over hers, he slowly lowered his cock to her leg. He knew she wanted it and also knew it would not be as pleasurable for her right now if he took her quickly. He teased her by pressing his cock onto her thigh. At last, he guided himself into her. Slowly he eased into her tight pussy. She was so wet for him. He groaned in appreciation as he sank slowly into the beauty that was Kelsey. He didn't know if he was going to last long, but he was going to try. He gave into moans as he slid deeper and deeper into her until finally he could go no further. She moaned and bucked, as he slowly established a rhythm that drove them both wild. He was going to ask her if she would come again when she loudly announced, "Jason, I'm going to come!"

He moaned and responded by pumping himself into her as they both exploded together. He collapsed onto her. She threaded her fingers into his hair.

"Jason, that was amazing. You are amazing."

"Kelsey, I feel exactly the same way. You blow my mind"

They feel asleep in each other's arms while Jason's body was still partly merged with Kelsey's.

24

They woke the next morning wrapped in each other's arms. Jason did something he hadn't done in years – took the morning off. It had been a long time since he'd felt anything like this. Come to think of it, Jason didn't think he'd ever experienced this sort of distraction. It couldn't be love, yet, but he was definitely in a deep state of like. With the way he was feeling right now, he wasn't sure his primal needs for her could ever be sated. Just then, Kelsey opened her eyes.

"Good morning," she said sleepily, covering her eyes with her hand against the sun streaming in the window.

"Good morning, yourself," Jason said to her.

He was propped on one elbow over her, and, now that she was awake, he gently stroked her hair. She smiled and started to kiss his hand. Jason smiled at her.

"Are you thinking what I'm thinking?" he asked.

She responded by lifting the covers off of her body. With her breasts slightly swollen from all the attention they'd gotten the night before, she looked all the more delicious to him. He reached out and gently caressed her breast. She moaned in appreciation. He caressed his thumb over her nipple and realized he didn't possess the patience he had last night. He would do his best not to rush it, but his cock was rock hard. As he positioned himself over her, she gasped again at his size. He looked down at himself.

"What?" he asked.

She smiled shyly, and her only response was wrapping her hand around his girth. It was his undoing.

"God, Kelsey, what have you done to me?"

She bit her lip with a coy smile and rolled over to her nightstand to get another condom. That would be their fourth wrapper on the floor. They didn't get much sleep through the night. Jason quickly opened the package of the condom and put it on. He gasped when he saw her touching herself in anticipation. He couldn't help himself, He had to have his tongue there once he saw her hands there. She continued to spread herself open for him while he lowered his face to her and gently started to lick her. She kept lifting her bottom off the mattress, and he decided to just tease her by brushing his finger over her bottom.

"Yes," she moaned.

Jason marveled at how deliciously dirty his Kelsey was. He let his tongue trail down to her bottom and ran it over her asshole. She moaned and urged him to continue. He licked his finger and just pressed it up against her. He darted the tip of his index finger in and out of her lightly. She responded by moaning loudly, and he loved every little sound she made.

"Jason, get your mouth back on me, please. I want to come for you," she finally said.

He obliged her. She had gotten so wet when he'd played with her bottom. He loved the way she tasted. He ran his tongue up and down her clit. She screamed his name as warm juices flowed from her. Jason plunged his hard cock into her. She bucked her hips.

"Fuck me hard," she said.

It was all Jason needed. He did exactly that as she ran her fingernails down his back. He had his mouth on hers while he was driving himself into her, and he exploded more powerfully than each time he had the night prior. He collapsed beside her, and they both erupted into laughter when they saw the time. It was after noon.

"I have to go to work, Jason. I hope no one there asks what I was doing last night."

"This may be our little secret for now, but I'm not sorry. This is the first time I've missed a morning of work in…well… probably ever. It was worth it."

A little while later, after one more lovemaking session in the shower, they both left her house together.

"So you work all weekend?" asked Jason.

"Yeah. I never thought my work schedule was a problem until now."

"Well, we will just have to talk on the phone every day and make it work".

"Sounds like a plan," said Kelsey.

They kissed goodbye, and, as Kelsey drove to work, she really hoped she didn't have that glow that is sometimes associated with sex and romance. If she did, she was in trouble.

25

Kelsey got to the bar a few minutes late and was thankful that Adam had already gone home for the day. She was glad that it was Friday night because any other day of the week she'd have stars in her eyes and probably mix up orders all night. She didn't have time to have stars in her eyes on a night as busy as a Friday. During the holiday season, Fridays were even busier and for that she was thankful.

She also didn't have time to think of all the trouble she'd cause the family if they found out. The moments she did have to spare, all she could do was think of all the lovemaking she'd shared with Jason the night before and earlier today. The thoughts alone were intoxicating. The more she reminisced, the more she could feel herself falling for him. She knew it wasn't safe to develop feelings too strong for him right now, but her heart seemed to have a mind of its own. Being consumed with thoughts of Jason also allowed her the luxury of not giving too much thought to Adam or Jesse finding out about them.

26

For a week and a half, Jason and Kelsey could not get enough of each other. On days that Kelsey worked, Jason always showed up at her apartment with a Bruegger's everything bagel (her favorite) and a steaming cup of coffee to go with it. He usually came at around 10 a.m., which was perfect timing for both of them. He'd completed all his morning appointments; she'd just gotten out of bed. This morning he came in with a bagel for himself, too, and they looked at each other adoringly and lightly conversed while they ate.

"How's it going at work?" Jason asked.

"Fine. No one is any the wiser, it seems. The holidays are a blessedly busy season, which means that Adam hasn't had too much time to talk to me. Right now, that seems to be working for me. How's it going with your big real estate developers?"

"Well, they're breathing down my neck about Dubicki's. I've been giving them the answers they want, but soon they will start demanding a sale or they'll possibly threaten to pull out of the deal. I hope that's not the case. I'm starting to fear that my relationship with you is clouding my sense of right and wrong in this case."

"I don't know what to say, Jason. I'm sorry that this is causing you stress. But I'm not sorry that the investors are not getting what they want right now, obviously."

He could tell she was angry. He could see that spark in her eyes. He was frustrated at the irony of it all, too. He reached out to caress her cheek and she leaned in to him and sighed.

"I'm sorry," she said.

"I know," he said.

He scooted his chair closer to her, closing the gap between the two of them. He leaned down and gave her a kiss. She responded by wrapping her arms around him and hungrily taking his mouth in her own. She unbuttoned his shirt and smiled when she saw his dressy trousers bulging. She unbuckled his belt then unfastened his pants. She got down on her knees between his legs and rubbed her hand over his erection. He helped her by lifting himself just slightly and sliding his pants off. Kelsey looked down at him and noticed the tip of his cock was glistening in anticipation of what was to come. She reached down and rubbed her finger over it. Jason watched in a trance as she raised her finger to her lips. She gently put her finger in her mouth and sucked it. Jason moaned. She responded by lowering her head back down to him. She teased him a little by kissing the inside of his thighs and his belly. She lowered her position just a little so she could gently lick his balls. He laced his fingers in her hair. She took the tip of her tongue slowly from his balls up under the length of his shaft. He responded by raising his hips slightly. She slowly took him into her mouth. Jason moaned.

"Kelsey," he whispered, as she continued to suck him hungrily.

He laced his fingers into her ponytail and gently guided her into a position he liked to urge her on, and she started to grind her hips and moan as she sucked him.

"Kelsey, I'm going to come soon. If you don't want to

take it in your mouth, you don't have to."

Kelsey didn't say a word when he announced he was coming. She took every drop of him into her mouth and swallowed greedily. Jason fell back into his chair.

"You blow my mind, Kelsey. Every time I think I know what's going to happen, you do something that surprises me. In a good way."

Kelsey got up and smiled as she went into the bathroom to get some mouthwash. She came back and put her arms around him as she sat in his lap.

"Would it surprise you if I wanted more?" she asked.

She had a condom in her hand, and just feeling her bare bottom on his lap was enough to make him swell with anticipation again.

"You're going to be the death of me, Kelsey, but, if that is true, I will die a happy man."

She smiled appreciatively as she lifted herself over him and slid Jason inside of her. He loved the way she felt. As he watched her beautiful body move up and down, he was taken with her beauty. She looked so amazing as her breasts bounced up and down and she rode him. He tipped his head back and moaned as he lost himself in her.

27

Saturday before work, Kelsey explained to Jason that she really needed to catch up on some Christmas shopping. He asked if he could go with her, but Mimi had been bugging Kelsey for details about her relationship with Jason. She realized that she missed her best friend and girl talk. Mimi was still the only person she could confide in about their relationship.

Mimi was buzzing with visible excitement when she saw Kelsey. They embraced and gave each other big hugs.

"Okay, first let's discuss the shopping game plan. Who do you have to buy for?" Mimi asked.

The two of them sat at a table in the food court and charted the stores they wanted to go to and who they wanted to buy for. In about 15 minutes, they had it all mapped out. They were efficient and task-oriented shoppers when they needed to be.

"So, now that we have that out of the way, tell me all about Jason! You have that shiny glow of happiness that normally makes me want to roll my eyes because I'm still single. Your happiness is almost contagious, though. I love that you are so happy! Let's walk and talk," Mimi said.

They set off on their Christmas shopping spree, and

Kelsey was impressed that they seemed to be making record time. As they shopped, Kelsey filled her in on the details of her relationship with Jason. Sex included. They were best friends, after all.

"Wow, Kelsey. It sounds like he's a keeper. But one day the bomb will drop when Adam finds out, and I hope this relationship survives it. I don't mean to be a downer, but you can't keep your head in the sand forever," Mimi said.

As they continued on their Christmas Shopping mission, Mimi told her all about the antics of the various men who approached her. When you looked like Mimi, that was pretty much a daily occurrence. Mimi was a great story teller. Kelsey often told her she should write a book.

"You should have seen this dude that approached me the other day. He had a gold tooth for one of his two front teeth. It was not happening," Mimi chuckled as she reminisced.

They decided to stop and grab some hot cocoa on their way out of the mall. As they juggled their shopping bags, they gave each other another hug.

"So, Kelsey, don't be a stranger. I know you've got Jason now, but you're going to have to introduce me to him one of these days."

"Well, I hope by the time that you two meet that our secret is out, along with a resolution to the business deal and whatever impact that our relationship has on that deal," Kelsey said.

"Uh, yeah. Good luck with that. You are in trouble, you know?" Mimi asked, shaking her head.

"What do you mean?"

"Hello! Any moron could see that you're in love."

Kelsey gasped at this revelation. Her hand flew over her mouth as her eyes widened with surprise.

"Well, I guess there's one person who doesn't know you're in love," Mimi said. "You."

"Wow. I didn't realize it, but I think you might be right.

I couldn't figure out what these emotions were. Duh. I guess a girl can't recognize them when she's never felt them before, so I didn't know it. I'm in love!"

They both jumped up and down before they hugged each other goodbye. Kelsey was glad she'd gotten most of her Christmas shopping done today, but she missed Jason. She smiled with the realization that she was in love and was thankful for Jason's presence in her life, no matter how he would be perceived by her family.

28

Kelsey arrived at work a little early. She was smiling. She was in love. As she started to prepare for her shift, organizing and stocking items around the bar, Adam came in from the back.

"Kelsey, can you come back here for a minute?" he asked.

She quickly finished wiping the counter down and walked back to the office. Adam had his arms crossed, and the look he gave her said something was wrong.

"What's going on, Adam? Is everything all right with Stephanie and the baby?"

Adam exhaled sharply. He tried to control his anger as he spoke.

"Really, Kelsey? Why don't YOU tell me what's wrong with me?" Adam said in a tone that suggested Kelsey knew what the problem was.

Kelsey blinked.

"Adam, I have no idea what you're talking about."

"I decided to give you the benefit of the doubt the first time I heard one of my friends say they thought they saw you with Jason Rourke. Then, one of our vendors was curious about it the other day. He told me he was sure he'd seen the two of you together on a romantic carriage ride in the city. What are you *doing*, Kelsey!"

"I'm sorry, Adam," Kelsey began and started to cry. "I know agreeing to go out with him was wrong. I just haven't felt an attraction like that, and I couldn't ignore it. He asked me out, and I went, even though I knew that if you or Jesse found out you would not be happy. We've seen each other a few times, and Adam, I really love him."

"Kelsey, I can't believe you took it upon yourself to make a decision like that without consulting this family. *We're* your blood. What would Dad or Dziadek say if they were still here? I know that who you date is your choice, but the minute you decided to pursue a relationship with the enemy of the Dubicki family, it became about the family. You should have told us!"

Adam balled his fists and walked over to his desk. He was so upset that he knocked a few of the papers off the side of the desk in frustration. He turned around and continued.

"The fact that you couldn't tell us about it for weeks is proof that you knew it was wrong. You are putting us in a more vulnerable position for losing Dubicki's. You should know that. He probably just used you to get his way with us. Did that thought ever once occur to you?"

Kelsey inhaled sharply at that accusation, feeling like she'd been punched in the stomach. She couldn't believe that Jason would use her. But what if it was true?

"I am very angry with you, Kelsey," Adam said. "I am also going to tell the rest of our family. You had better hope that Jesse doesn't take off and give Jason a piece of his mind."

That would likely consist of Jessie pummeling Jason. Jesse was getting very close to becoming a professional MMA fighter. A move like that could hurt his career. And hurt Jason. She couldn't let that happen. She had already been sobbing, but she cried all the harder.

"I'm giving you the night off to decide what you are

going to do. It's us or him, Kelsey. I'm sorry, but there's no other way."

Kelsey could barely see through her tears as she grabbed her purse and coat and ran out of the bar into the harsh afternoon light.

29

A half box of tissues and one pint of Haagen Dazs Chocolate Chocolate Chip ice cream later, Kelsey picked up the phone to call Mimi. All she had to say was that the family found out, and Mimi ditched her own plans. Twenty minutes later, Mimi showed up at the door with a bag of Chipotle tacos and a bottle of tequila. This was their tradition in times of crisis, and it was clear why Mimi had brought it tonight. Kelsey pushed the thought of the hangover she'd have tomorrow to the back of her mind. She was grateful that her friend had come to the rescue and that her best friend had her back.

Three shots of tequila later, Kelsey got the story out with her shot glass on one side of her and box of tissues on the other. They were sitting at the kitchen table, which they only did when there was enough drama in their life to do shots.

"Okay, Kelsey, I love you. I support you no matter what, and you know that," Mimi said as she hiccupped. "But you knew you'd have to face the music at one time or the other. Putting your head in the sand didn't mean it wasn't going to surface. Now what are you going to do?"

"At some point during the pint of ice cream, I made

my decision. I can't turn my back on my family and should have never allowed this to happen. What if Jason was using me, anyway? I'll never know the truth, and I don't know if I want to find out."

Mimi hugged her and told her she was sorry. There was just no happy ending for Kelsey, no matter which way she sliced it. They commiserated over some chips and guacamole paired with another shot of tequila. After that, they were exhausted. And drunk.

The next morning, they both woke up feeling like they'd been hit by a bus. They started to point and laugh when they each saw the other. They both took a turn quickly getting ready. It was their tradition the morning after tequila shots to go as is to breakfast for waffles. That could mean that they had to go with smeared mascara and hair sticking up, but it was their tradition. They always laughed their way through the waffles. A couple of hours later, she and Mimi parted, leaving Kelsey just enough time for a quick nap and another cry before she headed to work.

30

Kelsey managed to keep her head at work and consoled herself by listening to music filled with angst and heartbreak for two days before Jason tracked her down. She'd been avoiding him and having to tell him her decision. That night as she left work, Kelsey couldn't wait to get home and go to bed. She'd been comfortable with a late night routine of ice cream and a Lifetime movie. When she arrived at her door, she groaned. Jason was standing on her porch. The time had come for her to face her fate and tell him it was over.

"Hi, beautiful," Jason said as she walked up. "I haven't heard a word from you for the last two days, so I decided that instead of imagining every possible heartbreak scenario in my mind that perhaps I'd come over here so you could talk me out of it."

Kelsey stayed quiet and unlocked the door, letting Jason in behind her. She turned to him, afraid that her feelings would betray what she had to say. She found it hard to just flip a switch and stop loving him, but still she knew she had to do this for her family. She'd always have the doubt that he'd used her in the back of her mind if she continued, anyway. She could do this. Resolved, she sighed and turned to face Jason. His eyes searched her face. He reached out to her, but she flinched. That's when he knew.

"Kelsey, what's wrong?" he asked.

She saw a tear forming in his eye and hated herself for what she was about to do.

"Jason, I'm sorry. I made a mistake. There's no way we can do this." Her lip quivered as she said it, and she was looking down at her feet.

"Did your family find out, Kels?"

"Adam found out, and he was furious," she told him as she nodded. "He also mentioned something which had never dawned on me. He said that you were probably using me. Were you using me, Jason?"

Jason took a step towards her and tried to put his arms around her. Kelsey resisted and kept her arms crossed around her chest. Jason stepped back and looked at her with shock and disappointment.

"I can't believe that you would think that, Kelsey. You knew what a risk this was for me. You're not the only one who had to make a sacrifice. I've never showed that side of myself to anyone, and now you want to throw it all away? I wanted this. I wanted us. I wanted a future, Kelsey, for the first time in my life. But now you're insinuating I may have used you, and I don't know if I can live with that. Not only because it's not true, but because I thought you were better than that. Perhaps you're not the person I thought you were, after all. I was starting to fall for you, but I want to thank you for setting the record straight. You'd better tell your brothers to hire a lawyer. You were the only thing standing in my way of pressing this deal. Now there's not a chance that your family has against me and the powerful investors I have behind me. Now it's going to be my personal mission to force Dubicki's out. I hope you're happy."

Jason turned on his heel and walked out the door.

Kelsey stood there in disbelief. Just like a child has a

delayed reaction when they get an injury, she stood there for a moment and then it hit. She howled as she never had before, and she knew that no ice cream, movie, or even a bottle of tequila could do the trick tonight.

31

Jason was mad. Mad at Adam Dubicki for going after Kelsey for this, and madder still at Kelsey Dubicki for accusing him of using her. Tears in the corners of his eyes betrayed his fury. This night was turning into a disaster. He should have known better than to think that love was possible. His mom had broken his heart long ago when she left his father and married another man. There was a little boy in him that was very cynical in regards to love.

He had wanted the things he saw others had, but he never knew how he'd find that one person until he met Kelsey. He had thought this was it. He had thought that she was the one. He was wrong. He turned up the car stereo and loudly played The Clash. In his opinion, music by The Clash could make any situation seem better. He didn't realize that the speed of his car seemed to mirror the speed of his thoughts. He nearly rear-ended someone twice. He had to get a hold of himself.

One good thing about this was that now he didn't have the distraction of the relationship to worry about. It would give him time he didn't have when he was focusing on Kelsey. Still, he was mad at her for giving up. Mad at himself for asking Kelsey Dubicki out in the first place.

What was he thinking?

He would channel his anger to help drive this business deal to the outcome he wanted. The Dubicki's wouldn't even know what hit them. Before, this had all been business. Now it was personal, too.

32

Days passed and Kelsey was in a daze. Whenever Adam tried to address her, she ignored him. If he was talking business, she was civil and did what he asked, but he didn't dare say anything else to her. She'd told him she made her decision and that her decision was the family, but she hadn't spoken to him since.

Tears welled up in Kelsey's eyes every time she thought about wrapping presents. When she went to wrap them, she just sat there looking at the things she'd gotten for Jason. She would have to return them, and she wished she had a receipt for their relationship and could return that, too. And the emotions that went with it. Sadly, life wasn't so easy. She wondered what she'd done wrong to deserve something terrible like this. Regardless, she was settling very comfortably into her melancholy routine.

This breakup had sucked the life out of whatever was left of Kelsey's holiday season. She'd be glad for the distraction of work and the fact that people always wanted to drink near the holidays for one reason or the other. It kept her mind off of her own problems, waiting on them and listening to their stories. She was a bartender which meant people always loved to tell her their problems. For once, she didn't mind it. She'd even accept the occasional shot that was sent her way from a customer which she normally would refuse. She caught Adam looking at her as she did a shot of Jagermeister with a group of guys and looked back at him with a challenge in her eyes. He just shook his head and walked away. This holiday season couldn't be over fast enough. Kelsey came to understand why the suicide rate was highest during the holidays.

33

Jason needed a drink. Or a workout. He opted for the latter as he had been at the gym a lot lately. Working out helped get his aggression out and also passed the time without Kelsey. He wanted to think of her as the enemy, but he couldn't. It wasn't her fault she was in the family whose bar he was trying to buy. He also knew that the only reason that she thought he'd used her was because her brother had infected her brain with that lie. Part of him wanted to punch Adam Dubicki, and part of him would have done the same thing if she were his little sister.

He'd had other women approach him. Jennifer, his Cougar du Jour before Kelsey, had tried to call him several times. He just ignored her. No one was going to fix him right now, and he had come to the realization that his libido was still attached to Kelsey. Their relationship had gotten too deep too fast. He had never felt like that about anyone before, and a lot of good that did him. He'd lost her anyway. Now all that was left was to pull out all the tricks he had up his sleeve to get this business deal done. That meant that he would find a way to strong-arm the Dubicki's out of the building in which they'd built their family business. He knew he still had feelings for Kelsey, but business was business. Since Adam was the head of the family, and it was Adam who seemed to want to stand in between him and Kelsey, Jason would do what he had to do. Jason didn't get mad. He got even.

34

Kelsey missed Jason. She thought that, even if he had used her, she had still fallen in love with him. She just didn't know how to stop loving him. She had barely realized what love was when it was taken away from her. Jason Rourke had her from the time her eyes first met his. It was as if she could see into his soul. All she had seen was love in those eyes. She realized now that she had also seen her future there.

She craved his touch, his voice, his love. There was only so much ice cream a girl could consume. Only so many attempts she could make at various distractions. Nothing would take away her feeling of loss. Kelsey sighed and watched yet another Lifetime movie. If she kept this up, she was going to have to start acquiring a few cats and just accept her fate as a crazy cat lady. She hoped that wouldn't lead to her being a hoarder, too.

35

The phone rang at the crack of dawn. Kelsey woke with a start and rubbed her eyes. What time was it, and who was calling her at 8 a.m. when she had worked half the night before?

"Hello," she said groggily as she answered the phone.

"Kelsey, it's Adam. We are having an emergency family meeting at the bar in 30 minutes. Be there."

"But--"

"No buts, Kelsey. I know you're pissed at me, but this is serious and it's about the future of our family business. I'm not going to talk about how your relationship with Rourke fucked this family up. It will become crystal clear once you hear why I'm calling this meeting."

Kelsey sighed and got out of bed. She splashed some water on her face, tied her hair high up on her head in a ponytail, and quickly got dressed. How her life could go from being on cloud nine a couple of weeks ago to feeling like she was now at rock bottom was beyond her comprehension. She didn't see how this could get any worse, but something told her that if it were possible, it was about to get worse. She had better get a double espresso on the way in.

Her little brother Jesse was not a morning person, either. They were always the closest of the three siblings when they were growing up, mostly because Adam was older. Still, she thought that even if they all had been closer in age, she and Jesse still would have bonded more. Jesse and she used to tell the other kids that they were twins, and they even spoke their own language when they were kids. Some of the words that they made up they still used to this day. Someday when either one of them got married, they weren't sure how they'd explain their closeness to their significant others. Luckily no one was threatening to break up her and her unofficial twin right now. Not even Jason Rourke.

She and Jesse both grinned at each other with eyes that were squinting at the day light. They each had gotten the exact same thing as was their tendency when awoken too early: double espresso. They raised their cups in greeting to each other. Adam walked out from the back office with fast, hard steps. The kind of walking that said you were in trouble, like a parent that was after you for punishment.

"I don't know what you two are smiling about," Adam said. "Jason Rourke's company filed an injunction today with the county to force us to leave our property. He's doing it on the grounds that he's got developers that will grow business in this city but that he can't do so without our property. Since everyone else on the block has sold, he's got a case. It could take a month or two, but in February we could have to surrender all that our family built. Further, we would not get a dime for it. He offered us money, and since we refused now we could be forced. Are you happy, Kelsey?"

Kelsey blinked in surprise, not only at the injunction but at Adam's accusation. Jesse looked at her as if silently questioning her with his eyes. It was clear that Jesse didn't know but was about to find out. Kelsey looked down in shame. Jesse reached out and put his hand on her shoulder as if to tell her that whatever it was he'd still love her.

"Jesse, before you absolve her with your silent language, maybe you should hear what your sister did. Do you want to tell him, Kelsey, or should I?"

Kelsey just looked at him with tears in her eyes.

"Our sister got involved with Jason Rourke," Adam said.

Jesse's head snapped back as if he'd been slapped. He looked at her in question, and Kelsey nodded with her head hanging down in shame.

"Even worse is the fact that I had to find out about it through two other people."

Jesse looked at her, the anger growing in his eyes. That temper was one of the things that made him into one of the state's best MMA fighters, but that wasn't in Kelsey's favor right now.

"I have only one question for you, big sister. Do you love him?" Jesse asked.

Kelsey gasped in surprise at the question and reluctantly nodded her head, ultimately telling her brothers that she loved the man that was trying to get the city to take their business away.

"Oh, great. That's fucking great, Kelsey!" yelled Adam.

Jesse shot his arm out in front of Adam as if to stop Adam from advancing towards Kelsey.

"I'm not saying it's right, Adam," Jesse said. "I'm mad as hell. But I love my sister, and I trust that she would not do anything like that to hurt us. Isn't that right, Kelsey?"

Jesse looked at her, and, again, all Kelsey could do was nod through her tears, allowing Jesse to continue talking.

"Listen, Adam. I don't know the whole story. But I'm willing to give Kelsey the benefit of the doubt. Maybe it hasn't happened to me yet. But I don't believe you choose who you love. Love chooses you. Remember when you met Stephanie? Do you remember falling in love? Why don't you cut Kels a little slack here. Because it seems to me, she's suffering from a broken heart. Now you're making it worse by asking her to choose sides."

Adam didn't say a word. He clenched his fist, and his jaw visibly tightened. He walked over to the bar and grabbed a small bar glass. He put it upside down and slammed his fist into it. It was something their father used to do when he was angry, only their dad used to do it with a butter dish. Their father later told them he would go buy butter dishes at the dime store. When one of the kids upset him, as children often do, Dad would break a butter dish before he took it out on the kids. Their father always told them how many spankings that used to save them. The bar glass was just as effective, but it didn't shatter quite as nicely. Adam's hand was bleeding. He grabbed a white bar towel and walked back towards them as if nothing had happened.

"Well, Kelsey and Jesse, I hope you two can live with that when you are helping us clean out all that our family built when, not if, the injunction goes through. You can also help me pay for the lawyer we are going to have to obtain now to help us fight this. It may be futile, but we are Dubickis. And the Dubickis do not go down without a fight".

"Adam, I am tired of you treating me like you're my father," Kelsey said. "Our father is gone. I gave up my dreams to help you run the family's business. I had my life planned out. I was going to finish art school and become an illustrator of children's books. I put that on hold for you. Your dreams, your bar, our family."

Kelsey's face was red, and she was visibly shaking with anger.

"I could have told you about Jason, but I knew better than to imagine that you'd understand. What I had with Jason wasn't wrong; it was beautiful. Now I will never know what could have happened. You told me to choose, and I chose our family!" Kelsey yelled. "You're treating me like shit, and it makes me wonder if I made the right choice. I'm tired of your holier-than-though attitude, as if you have somehow been perfect. How dare you judge me!

How dare you accuse me of being disloyal to this family! Apparently, you can have it all: the wife, the kids, the family business. Jesse can even have his. But me, I have to give up everything to be in this family. Well, fuck you!"

Kelsey turned around with her fists balled and stomped out.

Adam took a step as if he were going to walk after Kelsey. Jesse held out his arm again and stopped him.

"Adam, leave her alone. You have done enough."

With that, Jesse made his exit to find his sister.

36

When Jesse found her in the parking lot, he held out his arms to her. Kelsey fell into his arms, turned her face into his chest, and cried some more. It felt good to give Adam a piece of her mind, but it didn't make her feel any better. She thought she could cry no more, but the tears seemed to have a life of their own. Jesse leaned his head down and kissed the top of his sister's head as she cried.

"Don't worry, Kelsey. I know this is difficult, but this will all work out. I don't know how or when, but it will."

Kelsey raised her head up to Jesse. He wiped the tears from her eyes.

"I hope you're right. You are the best little brother, and it means so much to me how you support me. I love you, Jesse," she said as she sniffled.

"I love you, too, big sister. I always have, and I always will. You know I'm not into praying, but I think if there was a time we could use Heavenly help, it would be now, so it's worth a try."

Kelsey nodded in appreciation.

They all went their separate ways. Kelsey was going to stop into church on her way home and light a candle. They all grew up in a Roman Catholic church, and her mother had always taught them to light a candle to the Blessed Mother in times when things seemed impossible. She couldn't think of anything that seemed more impossible than this situation, and she didn't know what else to do. Right then, she really missed her parents.

At the chapel, she put her money in the offering slot and took the long match to light a candle. She knelt on the kneeler in front of the statue of the Virgin Mary and prayed as if she were speaking to her directly.

"I know I've been wrong," Kelsey began. "I know I shouldn't have seen Jason or fallen in love when his company was trying to buy out our family business. Now my brother Adam is furious with me, we might lose our family business, and I feel like it's all because of me. Worse still, I miss Jason. I blame myself for the action he's taking with the injunction against us. I know it's not right. I know it might hurt us, but I still love him. Please help us. Help guide me in the right direction. I don't know if I can live without him, no matter how he's hurt me."

She put her head down on her hands which were folded in prayer. She didn't know if she believed in miracles, but, if there were ever a time when she needed a miracle, this was it.

37

Jason paced along the floor of his condo. The view of the city at dusk outside his floor-to-ceiling windows was breathtaking. He sighed. He was brooding. He pressed his fingers to his temples as if he were trying to make the pain go away and forget the last few weeks. She had made her choice. He wished her choice had been different, but that would not change things today. When she'd first walked away, Jason was crushed. But when he got down to the thick of things, he'd thought he was probably better off. He looked back now and wondered what happened to the drive that had always pushed his career. He should have filed the injunction against Dubicki's weeks ago, but he allowed the feelings he had for Kelsey to soften him. Now, he was back. Sadly, that didn't make him feel any better. It should have been easier to get over her.

What was it about Kelsey Dubicki that he couldn't seem to shake? The way she smiled at him. The way she always smelled like a breath of fresh air with a hint of lemon. It was intriguing, and he missed being near her. They laughed together and seemed to never tire of things to talk about, and, when they did have a silence, it was comfortable. Jason still marveled at that fact. He'd never known comfortable silence before her. Even in all of his business negotiations, there was always a tense silence during the process. How could she have infected him so deeply? He needed to move on, but he found his thoughts always drifting to her.

Jason's doorbell rang. He walked to the door wondering who on earth would be there; he wasn't expecting company. He opened the door to find a man he sort of recognized. Then Jason realized he'd seen the man at the door once on TV. This man had the same dark hair and eyes as Kelsey, and there was an added depth to his features. He was not overly tall, but what he didn't have in height, he made up for in width. *This man is built. Wow*, Jason thought. Jason seriously hoped he was not here to threaten him.

"Jason Rourke?"

"Yes."

"I'm Jesse Dubicki, Kelsey's younger brother. Can I come in?"

Jason hesitated for a moment and then nodded consent as he opened the door and gestured Jesse to come in.

"Kelsey and I have always been close," Jesse said. "When we were kids we used to tell other people we were twins. We're only a year and ten months apart, and it was hard for anyone to tell the difference in our age. When Adam told me about what had happened between the two of you, you'd think I'd be mad. For a moment, I was. But I love my sister and figured she would not do something like this without reason. I would give my life to protect her, and I needed to understand why she did this."

Jason nodded his head, urging Jesse to continue.

"I asked her one question: 'Do you love him?'" Jesse said.

Jason's eyes grew big in anticipation of the answer. He wasn't sure he wanted to hear it, one way or the other.

"Mr. Rourke, my sister was sobbing at the time because of all my brother had said. As you know, our family is not happy with you. I asked her that one question, and she nodded that yes, she loves you. That was all I needed to hear."

Love? Who said anything about love? Damn it, Jason thought. He paced again while Jesse stood there. Jason realized then that that's the answer he wanted to hear.

"So I'm here, Mr. Rourke--"

"Call me, Jason," he interrupted.

"I'm here, Jason, because my sister thinks she did something wrong. Kelsey is the one woman I know who would not knowingly wrong anyone. She loves you. My sister is more important to me than any business deal between our families. She deserves to be loved. Don't go after her because I made this speech. But if you love her, truly love her, then please fight for her. Isn't your future and happiness worth it?"

With that, Jesse turned around to leave Jason's condo. Jason followed him to the door, speechless.

"Thanks for your time, Jason. If you hurt her again, I won't be so kind next time."

Jason chuckled.

"It was nice to meet you, Jesse. Have a good night," Jason said.

Jason extended his hand to Jesse's, and they shook hands. Jason had a lot of information he had just been given to process. Was that why he couldn't get her off his mind? Was he in love?

38

Kelsey was in a deep sleep when her phone rang. She rolled over onto her stomach, grappling for the phone on her nightstand with her right hand. She burrowed her head into the pillow, not yet wanting to see the light and wondering who had the nerve to call her on her day off.

"Hello?"

"Kelsey, it's Mimi. *Wake up!*"

"It's my day off, and I don't want to wake up," Kelsey pouted.

Mimi knew Kelsey was a grouch when she woke up, so Mimi was not surprised that the greeting Kelsey gave was reminiscent of a porcupine. Just then, Kelsey heard the lock turn in the door and regretted ever having given Mimi a spare key. Mimi walked in and dragged the covers off Kelsey. Kelsey quickly recoiled into a fetal position, placing her arm over her eyes.

"What gives, Mimi?"

"Kelsey, it's 4 p.m. You should not be in bed this early. I know you've been hurting over the breakup and the drama with Dubicki's."

Kelsey was shooting arrows at Mimi with her eyes.

"Listen, Mimi, I love you, but don't judge. I haven't felt

well, and you don't know what I'm going through, so I don't want to hear it," Kelsey said indignantly.

"Oh, boo hoo. I'm sorry, girl, but I love you. I'm your best friend, and this is what you have me around for. I would be expecting the same from you, even though I'd hate you just like you probably hate me at this moment. You'll get over it, and you need to get out of the house and at least try to have a good time".

Kelsey crossed her arms stubbornly, but she reluctantly gave in. She knew that Mimi had a key to her place. That meant if she didn't do this, Mimi would never go away.

"Fine," Kelsey said curtly. "I need caffeine if I'm going to go out."

Mimi smiled with satisfaction and turned on her heel to go to the kitchen. As Mimi left the room, she called over her shoulder, "I'll make some nice strong coffee. But if you want more than one cup, the second is coming with a shot of booze. I'm just saying."

Kelsey groaned.

An hour later, they were ready. Kelsey was dressed to the nines. Somehow Mimi had gotten her to wear a push-up bra, which was annoying but made Kelsey feel remarkably sexy. She hadn't felt that way since she'd been with Jason, and that had been over a week. It seemed like an eternity. Mimi had done Kelsey's makeup, and although Kelsey would never admit it, she was glad because Mimi put on makeup like a professional. Model. Not a stripper. There was a fine line, but Mimi had good taste in being provocative without going too far. Of course Mimi had to put just a touch of red lipstick on Kelsey. Nothing over the top, just enough to make it look like Kelsey had sucked on a red popsicle a little too long and it had stained her lips. Kelsey's eyes had a touch of black eyeliner, beautifully smudged just to look fashionable and nothing more.

Mimi had brought a cute little club-hopping outfit that suited Kelsey's taste while stretching it just a little. Kelsey had on black slacks that hugged every curve. Skirts just weren't Kelsey's style, and Mimi knew it. Mimi had chosen a red lace camisole with a soft, classic black cardigan over the top. It wasn't a big cardigan but a form-fitting one that looked perfect with the outfit and black pumps. To top it off, Kelsey had a black clutch that matched her patent shoes. Kelsey did believe that she was looking good tonight, which was better than she felt. She was hoping the rest would follow.

They heard a honk outside and left Kelsey's apartment to get into a cab. Tonight they were going into the city: downtown Minneapolis. It was just far enough away from the people Kelsey knew, and downtown they could do some dancing and clubbing.

They paid a cover and entered a trendy new bar. It had several rooms that all looked like a lavish apartment with different living rooms. There were two bars at opposite sides and a dance floor in the middle. There were a lot of pretty people there, and it figured. But tonight Kelsey felt like one of them. It helped her get her mind off of her troubles for a while. She wanted something strong tonight and ordered a dirty vodka martini at the bar. It didn't take long for two guys to come and approach them. Although the attention was flattering, Kelsey wasn't interested. She sighed. This could be a long night.

39

It had been too long since Jason had been out, and he didn't feel like it now. But his buddy Lee had called, and he figured what the hell, it would get him out of the house. Lee liked getting away from his wife and kids every once in a while. Jason being single and having a condo in the city provided the perfect place for Lee to hang out, go party with Jason, and crash afterward.

They entered a trendy new club. Jason liked the atmosphere. It was a little more upscale, and the women there were appropriately upscale, as well. Unfortunately, he could care less about women at the moment, but that didn't mean he couldn't appreciate beauty from a distance. Jason and Lee sat down in one of the rooms that had a retro, late fifties feel. It almost had a beatnik style and sported a few lava lamps to add to that charm. They were on their second round when Jason recognized a familiar voice.

"Hi, Jason."

Jason turned around and saw Jennifer, his lover before Kelsey. Jennifer was a lonely suburban divorcee. There was a time not that long ago that Jason would have been happy to see her. She had a hot body and was always good to go. Unfortunately, Jason didn't even know if he could perform with anyone other than Kelsey, and, frankly, he didn't care to try. He was less than thrilled to see Jennifer right now, but she was coming toward him.

"Jason!" she exclaimed and reached out to hug him.

Jason turned around with a fake smile pasted on his face and let her kiss him on the cheek. He hugged her and returned the kiss on her cheek.

"I've missed you, Jason," Jennifer said in her husky, fuck-me voice.

She ran her finger down his neckline to where his chest was lightly exposed from the top two open buttons on his shirt. She presumptuously turned her little fanny around and sat in his lap. He didn't have the time or the energy to stop her. She started to whisper dirty things in his ear. He didn't know how much more he could stomach. He missed the touch of a woman, but not this woman. Still, he didn't have the energy to push her away. He let her nuzzle in his neck for a minute, but he knew he had to let her down soon. He couldn't go this far with her, or anyone right now, until he cleared his head.

Just as he was thinking about getting up, Jason heard a glass shatter. He turned to see what had created the commotion. It was Kelsey, who had been passing by and dropped her glass when she saw him. When Jason realized it was her, he quickly pushed Jennifer from his lap and jumped up. Kelsey was just standing there, frozen, looking at him and Jennifer.

"Kelsey!" Jason exclaimed and walked toward her.

He could not believe how this must look. Jennifer's timing had been terrible, and he should have refused her. Jason knew he missed Kelsey but hadn't realized just how much until that moment. She looked amazing tonight. In seeing her, he was overcome with the need to be near her. He started towards Kelsey, who still seemed in a daze from what she'd just seen. He had to explain and hoped she'd listen.

Kelsey's lip started to tremble, and she backed away from him. She didn't say a word. She picked up her purse that had fallen with the glass and she ran. Jason watched her go and reached to his pocket to pull out some loose bills. He threw more than enough cash on the table to cover his tab. He grabbed his coat and fought to get it on as he ran after her. He had to find her.

40

Kelsey thought she might be in shock. Then she realized she was in far too much pain to technically be in shock. Just when she thought she'd cried all she could cry. Just when she thought maybe Mimi was right about it being a good idea for her to go out and have a good time. Of all the clubs in the city, Jason had to be at this one. Really?

Not only was it shocking to see Jason, but it crushed her heart when she saw him with someone else; a cougar, no less. The woman looked like she was chauffeured in to the city from the well-to-do suburbs. Kelsey was mad. She felt like she'd been duped. Adam was right; Jason had used her.

She ran out of the club without her coat and without telling Mimi where she was going. She had to get out of there. She had to get home. She wiped the tears off the side of her face with the back of her hand and tried in earnest not to let her high heels slip on the icy cement sidewalk. Thank goodness there was a cab stand right there. She got into a waiting taxi and didn't look back. She couldn't wait to get home and get back into her warm pajamas and fuzzy slippers. Kelsey would text Mimi when she got home to let Mimi know she was safe. Then Kelsey couldn't wait to burrow under the covers and shut out the rest of the world for the night and most of the day tomorrow.

A half an hour later, Kelsey finally got in to her apartment. She was freezing because she ran out without her coat, but leaving it was worth her piece of mind. She put some water for tea in a pot to heat while she changed, and she sent Mimi a quick text explaining what happened and letting Mimi know she was okay. Mimi replied saying that she saw the whole thing and was sorry. Mimi would take Kelsey's coat for her and get it back to Kelsey later. Mimi apologized like it was her fault, but it wasn't. Kelsey wanted to scream at the world right then, but it still wasn't Mimi's fault for taking her out tonight.

As Kelsey changed into her fuzzy pajamas and slippers, she still couldn't believe what had happened. She had been so sure Jason truly had feelings for her. No one that loved her could be with someone else so fast. Kelsey had been sure Adam wasn't right. Not only did it hurt now, but it would hurt all the more when Adam said, "I told you so." As she thought about it and replayed the scene of seeing Jason with that woman over and over in her head, it made her cry all over again. She went to get her cup of chamomile tea and pulled out one of her favorite chick-flick movies to watch in bed.

She was all snuggled under the covers when she heard a knock on the door. She hit the mute button on the TV and pulled the covers up to her chin. Whoever it was, she didn't want to answer the door. She heard Jason's voice and jumped in surprise.

"Kelsey! Kelsey, are you there? Kelsey, it's Jason! Open up!" he called. "Kelsey, I'm sorry. That didn't mean anything, and I didn't mean to upset you tonight. Open up! Please, give me a chance to explain."

He continued for what seemed like a half an hour before giving up. It was a good thing the owner of the duplex she lived in was out of town for the holidays, or she surely would have been kicked out for all the noise. She wasn't ready to face Jason yet. She probably would never be ready. He broke her heart, and now he was taking the family business away. Add that to the fact that she had figured out that he had used her. No way! She didn't need anything like that in her life. Ever.

41

The next morning, Kelsey tumbled out of bed, groggy and worn, and made a strong pot of coffee. She looked at the clock and saw that it was almost noon. She felt like she had wasted the day. Then she remembered what happened last night and shook her head as if she could make the bad dream go away. The worst part of things like that was waking up the next day and having the nightmare hit you all over again. This was going to be a long day.

Christmas was only a week away. Kelsey hadn't felt this depressed during a Christmas season since her mother had died. She really missed out growing up without a mom for most of her life. She loved her family but really missed having her mom. It was a gap her dad or brothers could never quite fill. Growing up with a pack of men in the house toughened her in some ways and for that she was thankful. Still, she sometimes talked to her mother as if she were still there. Her dad had never been the same since her mother had died. Her mother had been the love of his life. He drank a little bit more each year after she died, and it was hard seeing her dad become more of an alcoholic as each year passed. He was a functional alcoholic, and it was easy for him to hide his problem because he owned a bar.

His children all knew, even if he was able to fool everyone else. It hurt the Dubicki kids, but like a good dysfunctional family, they never really talked about it. Perhaps if they hadn't enabled him by sweeping it under the rug they might have been able to save him. But deep down, Kelsey knew that what their father had was a disease. No one could have saved him but himself. It was his heart that eventually gave out. It was hard to let him go, but they all consoled themselves by saying he was with his sweetheart again in Heaven.

Now, with all that she was going through, she didn't really have anyone she felt she could talk to. Mimi was a great friend, but Kelsey barely knew how to put this into words herself. She wasn't ready to confide everything to Mimi yet. So she decided to get ready for work early and take a trip to the cemetery on the way. She missed her parents and always liked to imagine she could talk to them in times of trouble. It was easier to confide in the dead than it was the living.

42

Jason still couldn't believe he'd seen Kelsey last night. She looked gorgeous all dressed up like that, and it reminded him of just how much he'd missed her. Sometime between telling Jennifer to get away from him and chasing Kelsey all over the city, he had come to a realization. He was in love. He'd never realized until that moment what people were talking about when they spoke of the lengths that people would go for the ones that they love. He had thought all the movies about love were just stories that people had to make up just to make themselves feel better that they'd never found it.

Jason knew what he had to do. Not only did he have to win Kelsey back, he had to find a way to get the developers to build without acquiring Dubicki's. He could never live with himself if they took it. He loved Kelsey. The Dubicki family could very well end up becoming his own family someday, and he could never live with himself if he didn't try to work around this to save their business.

Three hours and a pounding headache later, Jason and his investors had come to an agreement. It meant that Jason would earn substantially less in this deal, but he got what he wanted. He didn't need the money and status that came with it. He needed Kelsey. Now it was time for him to find her and beg her to come back to him.

43

An hour later, Jason stopped by Dubicki's. He was initially greeted by a less than happy Adam Dubicki. Jason spoke to Adam and explained that he loved Kelsey and couldn't live with himself if something had happened to Dubicki's. Jason also told Adam he wanted to marry Kelsey. Adam blinked in shock. When it seemed Adam had finally processed all this information, Jason asked for Adam's blessing to marry his sister Kelsey. Adam agreed.

Now Jason was on his way to find Jesse at the gym, Jesse's second home to the fighting ring. As Jason entered the gym, he saw Jesse in the ring with who Jason assumed were Jesse's sparring partners and coaches. Jesse seemed to be made of sheer muscle. Jason was silently relieved that Jesse had come over to talk peacefully that night. He wouldn't want to be on this guy's bad side. As Jesse finished up and went to get feedback and confer with his coaches, he noticed Jason and walked over.

"Hi, Jason," Jesse said. "What brings you here?"

"I'm sorry to bother you during your training, but I wanted you to know how much it meant to me when you came by the other night. I didn't realize it at the time, but I'm in love with your sister."

"Hell, I knew that when I saw you. You have it bad for her," Jesse laughed.

"I'm stubborn sometimes, and I didn't realize it until she was gone. I miss her. I realized that there was no way that I could live with myself having a hand in destroying your family business because I love her," Jason explained. "I have to find her. I stopped by her place, but she wasn't there, and she's not at work yet. Last night, she saw me out with another woman."

Jesse's eyes darkened defensively as Jason continued.

"It wasn't what she thought. It was an ex of mine who threw herself at me. Kelsey ran out. I chased after her, but she wouldn't talk to me. I need to find her. I need to beg her for forgiveness and tell her she's the love of my life."

Jesse listened hesitantly.

"First, I need to ask you something, Jesse. I want to marry your sister, and I need the blessing of both of her brothers before I ask her because your father isn't here to give me that blessing. I've already been to see Adam and have his blessing."

Jesse was stunned. One minute Jason was explaining how he had upset Kelsey, and the next Jason was declaring his love for her and asking for Adam's blessing to marry her. If this was love, Jesse wanted no part of ever being in love. But he was happy for his sister.

"You have my blessing, Jason, as long as that's what Kelsey wants. What's important to me is that she is happy."

"Understood. I don't know what will happen when I find her, but I'm going to do everything in my power to let her know how I feel and beg her to give me another chance."

"Based on what you've told me, Kelsey's upset. If you can't find her and she's not at the bar, there's only one place she could be."

"Where's that?" asked Jason.

"The cemetery. When Kelsey is the most upset, she

goes to talk to my parents. Kelsey never got over missing having a mother. We all missed our mom, but it has always affected her the most. She wants to go put flowers on their grave and confide in the momma that she misses. It's the cemetery off of St. Anthony Parkway. You know the one?"

"Yes, I've driven by it several times. I'll go see if she's there. And, Jesse? Thank you."

Jesse nodded his appreciation at the comment and extended his hand to Jason.

"Good luck," Jesse said.

"Thanks. I'll need it."

Jason grinned as he left to go find Kelsey and declare his love.

44

"Mom, I thought I loved him. What was I thinking? I wish you were here to talk to me. I miss you."

A tear gently ran down her cheek. Kelsey leaned over and put the Christmas wreath she'd gotten for her parents down on their tombstone. She'd been pouring her heart out for the last half hour, and she was cold. She sighed and turned around because it was time to think about going to work. She blinked in surprise.

There stood Jason Rourke, watching her.

"What do you want, Jason? How did you find me?"

"Kelsey, I'm sorry. A thousand times, I'm sorry. I know that what you saw last night could not have been easy."

Tears ran down Kelsey's face. Part of her wanted to run, but part of her wanted to hear what he had to say. She stayed rooted in her position and lifted her chin to hold her head high and brace herself for whatever it was he was going to say.

"I had gotten so used to wanting to prove myself in business that I never had time for love before," Jason began. "I could barely acknowledge that romantic love existed. My life was all about business deals and being the best I could be. Then I met you. That first time I saw you, everything changed. I knew my life would never be the same, but I didn't imagine you'd touch me this way. It was not until last night that I realized that I'm in love with you."

Kelsey started to cry even more, and he held his arms out to her. She stepped into them and realized she was home. Jason kissed her on the top of her head and continued.

"This morning I realized what an ass I've been. I had to change things. I had to beg you to come back to me and tell you how I feel. Kelsey, I talked my investors into building around Dubicki's."

Kelsey looked up at him and gasped.

"You did?" she said through teary eyes.

"Yes, I did. You taught me that life is not all about business deals, and there was no way I could live with myself if I had a part in taking Dubicki's from your family."

Kelsey reached up on her tip toes and offered her lips to him. He kissed her hungrily. He laced his fingers through her hair and made love to her mouth. She moaned. Finally, she came up for air.

"Jason, I love you, too."

Together, they walked hand in hand from the cemetery. Kelsey's feet felt like ice cubes, but she was beyond caring about her bodily needs at that moment. What her heart needed was Jason. Thank God he'd come back to her.

45

Kelsey woke up the next morning feeling refreshed. Feeling loved. Jason lay next to her, and she realized he'd been watching her.

"You're beautiful when you sleep," he said.

She responded by reaching up to him and pulling him down to her. She'd missed his touch and couldn't get enough of him. As he kissed her tenderly, he shimmied nearer to her underneath the sheet. They were already nude from all the loving they'd had the night before. He lifted the sheet up for just a moment; he just could not get enough of seeing her beautiful body. As he looked at her, she smiled a mischievous smile and lifted her body up in need. She softly parted her legs and started touching herself. Jason responded by leaning his head to her breast and teasing it lightly with his tongue. She moaned, and the rhythm of her fingers got faster.

He continued to lick both of her breasts and was contented watching her for a few minutes. He was rock hard and finally rose up on his knees to approach her. Still, she didn't stop touching herself, and his cock nearly erupted in anticipation. He lowered himself down to her pussy and replaced her fingers with his tongue. She moaned, loudly. Gently, he licked her sweet pussy and let his tongue wander down to her entrance. He darted it and out, then down further a bit to her bottom. He teased her there, and she loved it. When he finally felt he'd teased her enough, he raised his head back up to her clit and licked her until she exploded into his mouth. She tasted so good.

As the tremors continued through her body, he raised himself over her and entered her slowly. She responded by crying out, and he didn't know how long he could last. He let her tight pussy grip him. He started with a slow rhythm because he wanted to try to last for her. She closed her legs tight around him and said, "Fuck me, Jason."

God, he loved her. He responded with enthusiasm, and when that wasn't enough she yelled again.

"Fuck me, Jason!"

He let himself slam into her again and again as she screamed her release and her body erupted again. He let himself explode with her, and they collapsed into each other's arms.

They snuggled for a while until Kelsey went to make coffee. It was late morning but still worth every moment they spent making love. Jason came up behind her while she was at the coffee pot, and she responded to his touch. She turned around to face him, and they kissed.

"I love you," she whispered in his ear.

"Kelsey, I love you, too. I feel like you were what I'd been waiting for my whole life and didn't know it until now."

They made omelets and had a lazy morning together. It was Christmas Eve. Kelsey couldn't remember being happier on the eve of her favorite holiday.

"Jason, do you want to go to mass with me tonight? Our family always attends midnight mass, and I would love it if you would be there with us."

"I'd be honored, Kelsey. There's no place I'd rather be

on Christmas than with you."

46

A few hours later, Jason went home to change for the evening. The Dubickis always got together to have cocoa and cider and exchange one present on Christmas Eve. He was beaming with pride that Kelsey wanted him to be with her family tonight.

Jason looked down at the velvet ring box in his hand. After he'd left Kelsey's, he had stopped by a jeweler to shop for a ring. When Kelsey asked him to be with her family tonight, he knew he'd likely propose sometime before Christmas was over. He wasn't sure exactly what moment that would be, but he would know it was time when he felt inspired to get down on one knee. The beautiful two carat, princess cut diamond on a platinum band sparkled back at him. When he'd gone to the jeweler's store, he wasn't sure what to pick for her engagement ring until he saw this one. There was something about the square diamond that seemed so old fashioned to him. Kelsey seemed to him to fit with that. She loved tradition and valued the treasures of her family. He thought this ring would be perfect for her. He hoped she'd like it. And say yes.

After a wonderful meal with Kelsey's family, Jason felt

sated. He had never felt something so right in his life. He loved the family and found it sweet how they all took turns with baby Jack, Adam's son. Kelsey cooed over the baby, and Jack always smiled for her. She would make a great mother someday. His chest tightened at the thought that they would have a family together. Still, he had to ask Kelsey to be his wife, and he knew he would know when it was the right moment. He felt it was near but was not quite yet.

They all left in separate cars to drive to the Dubickis' church. Jason marveled at the beauty of the church as they got near. It was such a clear, beautiful night. As he and Kelsey stepped out of the car, it started to snow big, beautiful snowflakes. It seemed that the moment would never be this perfect again. This was it.

Jason took Kelsey's hand and led her over to the side of the church near the outdoor manger scene. She looked at him with a question in her eyes but followed him anyway. He turned and took both her hands in his.

"Kelsey Dubicki, I believe that we were meant to find each other. I had no idea what love was until I'd realized how deeply in love I am with you. Your love is the best gift I've ever received."

He reached his right hand into his pocket and got down on one knee. Kelsey gasped and put her hand over her mouth. The snowflakes continued to lightly fall around them. He opened the box and took her hand as he began to speak.

"Will you marry me?"

Kelsey cried and nodded her head.

"Yes!" she answered.

Jason slipped the ring on her finger. They embraced each other and kissed. A small crowd had stopped behind them, including her brothers and family. The whole family came forward to congratulate them. Kelsey and Jason held hands while they all walked into church together as church bells rang twelve times signaling Christmas had arrived.

EPILOGUE

Kelsey woke up with a smile on her face. She was truly starting to love mornings. Ever since she had found out she was pregnant a few weeks after Christmas, she had been filled with hope by the love and family that she was in the process of creating. Jason had been just as surprised as she had been about the pregnancy. Their reunion on Christmas Eve was so passionate that they had forgotten to use a condom. They'd both hoped to approach marriage and family a bit more in the traditional order of things: Marriage, then family, but they agreed that they were blessed to be able to start a family together and both felt that they couldn't be married fast enough, anyway.

They had decided on a Memorial Day Weekend wedding. It was the perfect time for spring to have awakened most of the flowers, trees, and grass. And the perfect time because with Memorial Day weekend they could honor Kelsey's parents, who she would miss on her wedding day. Her father had been in the Army. Memorial Day in the United States was traditionally a day to honor lost loved ones who'd served in the armed forces, but it was also a day to honor all lost loved ones, and Kelsey liked that. As Kelsey had her morning tea, she decided that before her wedding she needed to go see the grave of her parents. She knew they weren't there physically, but she still felt she needed to get close to them and have some sort of spiritual blessing from her mom on her wedding day.

She pulled into the cemetery and marveled at the bright sky and the birds singing their spring song. She walked to her parents' grave and placed roses on their headstone. A tear gently slid down her cheek. Her bottom lip quivered with emotion as she began.

"Hi, Mom. Hi, Pop. It's my wedding day. Something tells me that you already knew that, but I needed to come here to tell you anyway. I met the love of my life. I don't know how it happened. It was rough at the beginning, but still it seemed it was destined. I never believed in that kind of stuff until this happened. Jason proposed to me on Christmas Eve, and a few weeks later we found out I was pregnant. I know that the way this happened is a little backwards, but we are both over the moon with joy. I miss you, Mom. I have so many questions about pregnancy. Jason's mom is great, and I'm so grateful to have her around, but sometimes it makes me miss you more.

"Today is my wedding day. Jason and I made our wedding day this weekend to honor the fact that you are gone, and we want to remember you on our wedding day. I'll miss you so much, Mom. Pop, I'll miss that you can't walk me down the aisle. We haven't told anyone this, but a few weeks ago we found out our baby is a girl. We both cried when we heard the news. We wanted a girl and are really excited. I hope she looks like you, Mom. I miss you both, love you more than you know, and hope you will be with me in spirit when I walk down the aisle."

Kelsey made her way back to her apartment. Mimi had just pulled up with her hair up in rollers, bridesmaid dress, makeup bag, and some sort of baked goods that Kelsey couldn't wait to see what they were. Kelsey had had a monster sweet tooth since she'd been carrying the baby. Mimi hugged her, and they made their way inside.

"So, how are you feeling?" Mimi asked. "It's your wedding day!"

Mimi took down two champagne flutes and made herself a mimosa with champagne and Kelsey a virgin mimosa with no alcohol. They toasted. Kelsey's eyes sparkled as she sipped her drink.

"I feel wonderful. I went to the cemetery. The weather is so great today. It's like Heaven is smiling at down at us."

They spent the next several hours getting ready. The other two bridesmaids had arrived shortly after Mimi, and they were all working on each other. Mimi had hired a makeup artist and hair stylist to help. They were all starting to feel fabulous as their look came together.

At last, Kelsey was ready. She looked at herself in the mirror. She smoothed her hand over her belly knowing that there was a miracle living within her. She felt like a princess in her floor length, chiffon, spaghetti-strapped dress. It flowed and made her feel like a bride without overdoing it. Her veil was waist length. It was a light layer of tulle that was corded on the sides. She liked the classic feel of it. Her eyes swelled with emotion, thinking of all she had gained. And all that she missed with her parents not being present.

Mimi gently interrupted her reverie by lightly placing her hand on Kelsey's arm.

"Kelsey, it's time to go."

Kelsey smiled and hugged her friend. The limo was outside that would take them to the church.

Kelsey entered the church. She loved hearing the organ music. They'd had a choice of hiring outside musicians but had chosen to stay with the traditional sounds of the church. She loved the feel and the smell of the church. She knew that there were blessings on them this day.

As the procession started, she watched her and Jason's close friends and relatives walk down the aisle arm in arm.

It was finally Mimi's turn. Mimi looked so gorgeous in her purple straight line gown. She smiled at Kelsey, placed her hands on her bouquet of yellow roses and proceeded down the aisle alone. Kelsey had wanted it that way to give Mimi a place of honor in being Maid of Honor.

The procession was complete, and the music shifted. Pachelbel's *Canon in D* began, and Kelsey felt a swell of emotion. She looked to her left and saw Adam. He kissed her on the cheek and grabbed her left arm. She looked to her right at Jesse and started to cry.

"There goes my makeup," she said.

Jesse chuckled and kissed her on the check.

"Don't worry, big sister," Jesse said, grabbing her right arm. "This is your day, and you look beautiful."

With both her brothers on each side, she began to walk towards her fiancé. More tears flowed as she saw her beautiful man. Jason looked so handsome in his classic black suit, white shirt, and tie. *How did I get so lucky?* she wondered. She was overwhelmed with emotion as she walked down the aisle, arm in arm with each brother, towards her future. She couldn't wait to become Mrs. Rourke.

The day wouldn't have been complete without the new Mr. and Mrs. Rourke making a stop at Dubicki's on their way to their reception. The bar was closed today for the family event, but Adam wanted to open it up for them and their wedding party to stop and have a few moments to themselves on the way to the reception.

As Jason and Kelsey pulled up to Dubicki's, Jason took her hand.

"Just think. This is where it all started. I could never have imagined meeting my future wife here, and now I couldn't imagine my life without you and all of the Dubicki family in it."

Kelsey dabbed the tear that was forming in her eye and took her husband's hand. They crossed the threshold of the bar into the warmth of her family and friends. She was proud to be a Rourke now and to be part of Jason's family. She was also proud to be the third generation of Dubickis that ran their family business, and hoped there would be many more generations to come.

THE END

ABOUT THE AUTHOR

Gabriella Scott lives near Minneapolis, Minnesota, with her three cats. In addition to being a an author, she is a voracious reader who loves good stories. Gabriella is also a musician - she sings and plays piano. When she is not playing with a band, she is usually out seeing one.